What was I supposed to do!

FROM THE PEN OF
Ni'cola

ISBN: 9780578937526
Library of Congress: 2021913975
First Printing 2021

This is a work of *fiction. It is not meant to depict, portray or represent any particular real persons. All the characters, incidents, and dialogues are the products of the author's imagination and are not to be construed as real. Any references or similarities to actual events, entities, real people, living or dead, or to real locales are intended to give the novel a sense of reality. Any similarity in other names, characters, entities, places, and incidents is entirely coincidental.*

Cover Copyright © 2021 by NCM Publishing. All rights reserved
Cover Layout & Design – Justin Q. Young
Editor – Keyoka Kinzy
Interior Layout & Design – Write on Promotions

NCM Publishing
www.IamNicola.com

Acknowledgements

This journey has been rough, but if it wasn't for my belief that there is a Heavenly Father above, I would not have made it this far. I thank Him for watching over me and continuing to open doors for me.

I would like to thank my family and friends again for continuing to have faith in me and believing in me. You guys are my biggest critics, and I appreciate the constant push. You continue to motivate and push me to keep this fight going. I wouldn't be shit without all of you.

Who would have thought that when I started the Girls Who Brunch organization that we would become a household name? I want to thank all the men, women, organizations, facilities, and schools nationwide that have joined forces with me to service over 25,000 girls!

To my entire Girls Who Brunch Tour Team, let's continue to make history and produce difference-makers throughout the world.

Dedication

This book is dedicated to all the amazing girls that I have met through Girls Who Brunch. I dedicate this book to you. All of you are beautiful, no matter what your circumstances are. As long as you have breath in your body, you have the ability to rewrite your story and be the best version of you that you can be.

I wrote this story because of all of you. I never wanted any of you to feel like you didn't know what you were supposed to do after meeting Girls Who Brunch. This story is for you.

To my Mommy, happy heavenly birthday. Thank you for being my biggest fan as a writer and slanging all my books. LOL. I love you, Queen. Rest well.

From the Pen of Ni Cola

Note to the reader

Peace Kings and Queens!

Being the founder of an organization like Girls Who Brunch I have the opportunity to work with so many different girls from many different walks of life.

Some of my girls are rescued from the sex-trade, some in group homes and foster care. Some of my girls are homeless and or victims of sexual and physical abuse while at the same time; some of my girls may come from homes that has great upbringings and wonderful support systems.

This book is a combination of real situations from real girls across the country. They are victims of being dealt the wrong hand and do not have access to positive options to correct the problems at hand. Through this book, I had one main objective: to give a voice to the voiceless.

Since slavery days, girls and women of color have always been oversexualized and over criminalized. They are usually the ones to get the harshest punishments at very young ages, without one thinking about how they got here.

When you read this story, I want you to do it with an open heart. Some of the situations are intense. Some of the characters points of views are difficult to accept, but they are all real.

These situations may cause triggers to physical and or mental abuse that you or someone you love may have endured, and I am apologizing in advance. But if it does, then I did my job.

Once you finish reading this story, I am asking all of you to take a moment and process what would you have done, if you were in Harper's situation.

What Was

I Supposed to Do?

Prologue

*M*ami? Mexico?

I laid on the couch with my head propped up on pillow, daydreaming about our nearing vacation. Once we came off this crazy ass lockdown, we were out of here! Stone had been very vague about the destination. The furthest place I had ever been was Cali when my Papa took me to Disneyland.

How old was I? Seven? Nine?

That shit was crazy! I ain't done nothing! After Papa had his stroke and ended up in that home, the only person I had was my crazy ass mama, and she never had any money! But that was about to change. Stone promised me the world and I was more than willing to take him up on his offer. The thought of traveling the world with that beautiful man made my heart flutter every time it came to mind. I was so lucky. Who would have ever thought he would have picked me to be his girl? Me! The half-breed mutt-girl, who ain't know who her own damn Daddy was could land a man like that?!

I was taking in my beautiful setting, listening to the Neo Soul station on Spotify and trying to learn some of the old songs that were playing. Neo Soul was Stone's favorite genre of music. I didn't want to appear as young as I was while we were on vacation, or once he started taking me around his family.

Lost in my thoughts, I did not hear the keys unlocking the front door. I was grinning from ear-to-ear when Stone entered the apartment, but my grin quickly faded when I realized that he had four guys behind him.

"Hey there, pretty girl," he said with a soft smile on his lips.

"Someone is happy to have me back home I see," he said, leaning in to brush a quick kiss against my lips.

I hurried up to pull the throw blanket up over my body. I tried tucking my body down behind the oversized pillows on the couch. I wasn't wearing anything but a pair of boy shorts and a sports bra. I didn't know he was going to bring company home with him. Stone hadn't brought anyone besides his sister, Denice, to the house, so I was totally caught off guard.

He must've sensed my nervousness. Stone gestured for the guys to take a seat in the dining room as he sat down next to me, rubbing my hand.

Even though I trusted this man with my life, the energy in the room was making me uncomfortable. The hairs on the back of my neck stood up and my body had a sudden chill.

"Pretty girl, these are a few of my friends. I told them about you, and they offered me top dollar to meet you," he said in a gentle baritone.

Top dollar? Did this dude just say what I think he said?

I shook my head, looking at Stone, then turned my attention to the men seated at the dining room table, cheesing like they just won the lottery. They looked the kind of guys Mama used to be on the corner with when I would go looking for her when I was little.

"Black, we can't see her, man. Gotta make sure she worth the five stacks," the pudgy one said.

He stood up, rubbing his hand across his crotch. I guessed he was waiting for me to get up.

My chills turned into a full-blown round of the shakes and my head started to hurt really badly.

OMG! Did he sell me to these guys? How much is five stacks? Five hundred or five thousand, and who the fuck is Black?

Not giving me an opportunity to speak, Stone grabbed my hand, looking me dead in the eyes.

"Don't embarrass me now, Harper," he said, exposing the gun at his waist with his other hand. "I need you to stand up, go to the guest room, and get into the shower. Leave on the towel and wait on the bed like a good girl.

When you are ready, call my name and I will send them in one-by-one. I need you to make them feel good, like you make me feel good. Okay? I have been bragging about you, baby. They just want to make sure that you are everything that I said you are. Now, be a good girl and do what I say. You hear me?"

Still holding my hand with a tight grasp, he pulled me slowly but firmly. The tears that had welled up in my eyes finally released and rolled down my face.

This man had claimed to love me and promised to never hurt me, but he really sat there, telling me that he sold me! He knew how I felt about pimps and prostitutes! He knew everything about me! *Why the hell is he doing this to me?*

Mama always said that if a man seemed too perfect, it was because there was a dirty secret he was hiding and needed his perfection to overpower it. After a while, his representative will go away and the real him would come out. I always blew her off when she spouted her hood parables, but right now, all of her words were ringing out in between my ears.

"Stop that shit, Harper. Now, go wash up. Make sure you use that smell-good body wash in there and wash your hair. Got to make sure you are fresh and clean for our guests, okay?"

He still spoke in his normal, soothing tone. Stone pushed me in the direction of the guest room, snatching the blanket from around me, exposing my barely clad body.

I knew that if I went into that room, I might never make it out because they were going to have to kill me before they raped me.

Did they know I was only sixteen?

I guess if it didn't matter to Stone, then it damn sure must not have mattered to them.

"Yea, my G. Her ass is fat like you said," the tall, light-skinned one said. "I got shotgun!" he exclaimed to the other guys at the table.

I wanted to scream and cry, but this was not the time for that. If I could pull this shit off, I could to do that later, but not now. Right now, I had to save my life.

I turned my attention back to Stone, trying to tune their voices out my head. Flashing him a soft smile, I turned all my feminine wiles on, hoping my pheromones would work in my favor at this moment. All my life, my mamma taught me the game that I had to use from time to time, but this was a moment when I had to pay attention and keep my cool if this shit was going to work.

"I got you, baby," I said before I leaned in to hug him and who would have thought? He opened his arms to embrace me, giving me a small window of opportunity to save my life. I hurried in and tugged the gun out of his waistband.

What the fuck!" he yelled, but I was too quick. I had possession of the gun, and the bad part about being raised in the projects and having a hoe for a mamma, I knew exactly how to use it.

Knowing from the weight and the bulge at the bottom, I knew it was loaded. I held the gun firmly, cocked it, and aimed it directly at Stone.

"Nigga, I thought you said she was with this!" the pudgy one yelled out to Stone.

"I am on papers and don't have time for no bullshit," he said, while inching towards the door.

The tall, light-skinned one stood up and said, "I am not going anywhere until I get some pussy or my bread back, period."

In that instance I knew, I was going to have to shoot and maybe kill someone tonight.

"Bitch! I told you not to embarrass me!" Stone hollered out, lunging towards me.

Stepping back, I took the shot, closing my eyes as the blast from the gun rang out in the air.

Harper

Buzzzzzzz. The alarm rang out as my cell doors opened. I really was not feeling that great, but I was happy to participate in anything that was going to allow me to be out of my cell for a few hours.

Officer Mead in Booking had an empowerment group that brought in speakers to encourage and enlighten us once a quarter. She told me about this when she was processing me into the system.

"You just missed the last event, but if you are still here, I will make sure to add you to the list," she said, flashing me a soft smile. I nodded my head and agreed to entertain her, not thinking I would really still be here. I just knew my mamma was going to come get me. My Papa was in that home, but if he knew that I was in jail, he would have made her come get me.

I totally forgot about Officer Mead and getting signed up until this morning. A guard I had never seen before in my unit came to my cell and told me that someone would be coming to get me around 1:45 p.m.

"Be on your best behavior," she said before walking off. "They have been in the gym all morning, decorating and stuff for y'all. The event got food and desserts. They're working really hard to do something nice, so you better act like you appreciate it. Okay?"

"Yes ma'am," I responded and laid back down. All I needed to know was that there was going to be food there and I was satisfied. I closed my eyes. 1:45

p.m. couldn't get here fast enough. My head and stomach had been hurting all day. I knew it was because I had not been eating enough here. The food was horrible, and I couldn't stand to eat it. I took in the bare minimum for nourishment, but it usually left me not feeling too well. I was going to try to sleep it off until it was time to go.

I stepped outside the doorway and automatically folded my arms behind my back, waiting for the guards to instruct me to move. I had been here for almost three months now, and I quickly caught on to this routine because I didn't want any issues.

Walking down the hallway towards the gym, it was still hard for me to process that I was really here. Every time I woke up, I took in a deep breath, blinked my eyes twice, and gave myself a moment to look around. Even though the walls in my home were concrete, because I lived on Donna in the projects, they were still more inviting to me than this place. The walls in my house represented a small thing that I kept taking for granted. My freedom.

At home, I had the freedom to come and go as I pleased. Even if our house was kinda fucked up, it was still ours. My momma pretty much let me do whatever I wanted to do. Even though my friends thought she was cool, I hated it. I wanted a mom who made me go to school, do homework, have chores. The only thing my Momma cared about was me disrespecting her boyfriend, James, and he was the main reason that I was here. SMDH.

The closer we got to the gym, I heard music playing.

Is there a DJ here?

I've never heard of an empowerment event that had a DJ. All of the ones I've been to in the past were at my Sidra's church. Now, they had music, but not a DJ. It was either the piano player doing a solo or the choir singing. Even though I didn't want to get excited, I was actually curious about what was going to happen and sped up my pace a bit.

I kept my hands folded behind my back even as I entered the gym. At first, this position was uncomfortable, but it soon became my peace. It was a silent, safe, reassurance blanket for me. If all of us had our hands behind our backs, I didn't have to worry about anybody trying to do something to me. Even though everyone here had been pretty cool, I could never be too careful. Some of the charges that these girls had, were way worse than mine, so there was no way I could trust anyone here.

"Hello ladies," I heard someone say into a microphone. "Please take a seat in the bleachers. We will be starting shortly."

Her voice was soft and inviting, not like any of the staff that worked here. Everyone here pretty much just barked orders and commands at us, so her voice was actually refreshing.

It wasn't until then that I realized how many of us girls were here. Some of them were following orders and heading towards the bleachers, while others were in awe by the decorations and the food. There were signs of girls having fun all over the place. There were balloon arches and columns everywhere. I knew that the officer said there was going to be food, but dang! They even had a fancy table with cupcakes and those chocolate-covered strawberries. All this for us?

"SIT DOWN!"

This time, it wasn't the woman with the nice voice. It was Officer Mead. She stood in front of the DJ, who turned down the volume of the music.

"Y'all need to hurry up, so we can start this event. These ladies do not have all day!" she barked.

If I was at home, I probably would have had a smart remark, but since being here, I had learned how to be humble and appear invisible. I didn't want any smoke with the officers. I wanted to be on my best behavior, so that I could get some of the food to eat.

Everyone was on the same page as me because it did not take long for us to get settled in the bleachers. The DJ turned the music back up, and that was when I realized this was more than just the DJ and the lady with the nice voice. There was a group of ladies seated behind the DJ.

Hmmm. What are they about to do?

It didn't take long for me to find out exactly what was going on.

"Peace! Peace! Peace, Queens! My name is Ni'cola Mitchell, and I am the founder of the Girls Who Brunch Tour."

Ni'cola? Hmmmmm, I like that name. It sounds exotic. I got so caught up on her name, I missed the question that she asked all of us. I saw the majority of the girls raise their hands, so I must have missed an important question. Hopefully, she didn't ask about the food.

"Red, raise your hand," Officer Meade bellowed out.

It didn't matter where I went. People always gave me that name because of my red hair and skin. My momma called me "Ginger," but everyone else called me "Red."

My grandpa told me a long time ago to never move with the crowd. He said that I should make sure I knew what I was being asked before I just followed the crowd, so instead of raising my hand, I did the next best thing.

"Can you repeat the question?" I asked,

Officer Mead had a look of disgust on her face, but Ni'cola smiled and repeated what she had said.

"How many of you are certified as adults?" she asked.

Ooooooo that was the question. Dang! I didn't know there were so many of us. I really thought it was just me, I thought to myself.

Slowly, I raised my hand and joined the crowd. Even though I was not sorry for what I had done, hearing it out loud always made me feel ashamed. I still could not believe that I had done this shit, but hey. It is what it is.

I expected Ni'cola to become nervous after learning this, but she did the exact opposite. She smiled at all of us. "I am, and I was you," she said softly, but firmly. She then began telling us her background. She had been raped a bunch of times, had her kids young, and was even brought to a place like this after a fight when she was younger. She was so transparent with her story that I had tears in my eyes. I didn't know what it was about this lady, but I promise you, I was beginning to like her.

The room was silent. Ni'cola told us all about her prior pain and trauma, but she confirmed she was still standing. She then explained all of her accomplishments. She had written mad books, ran this organization, and was even featured in Forbes

Magazine. I never actually saw Forbes magazine, but I knew that Kylie and Kim Kardashian had been featured there a bunch of times. I knew that this Ni'cola lady must have been kind of important.

As she spoke, her voice was so soothing that I just wanted to be her friend.

What did she say that her company was called? Girls Who Brunch? I definitely knew I was going to look her up when I got out.

When I first got to the event, I was so anxious to get some food. Surprisingly, I was disappointed when Ni'cola dismissed us to get some food, so that she could bring in the panel. I had tears welling up in the corners of my eyes because I really felt that she understood us. I hurried up to get my food, realizing how excited I was to see what the rest of the day was going to bring.

Christine

"What are we going to do?" I asked. My

hands wouldn't stop shaking as a pulled out another
Newport Slim to smoke.

The palpitations of my heart felt so intense. It
felt like at any moment my heart was going to jump out
of my chest.

The front door opened, and James came back in.
He sauntered his ass up the stairs in silence. I wanted
to cry. I wanted to scream, but instead, I didn't say

anything. Even though he had pissed me off so badly, I was happy to see him.

The spring evening was unusually cool for April, but I had the air conditioner turned all the way up on high. I was afraid of this virus thing. In my head, if I kept my house cold, I might have a fighting chance against getting sick. Goosebumps appeared on my arms and I attempted to rub them out.

It was my first time seeing this ninja since he had decided to stay at his house when this shutdown started, leaving me alone with my thoughts. It was his fault I didn't go get Harper out of Juvie. She said he hurt her, and I just could not see that shit! This man did everything for Harper, like he was her real dad. I just couldn't believe he would hurt a hair on her head, let alone rape my baby.

"James! What are you doing?" I yelled up the stairs. I could hear him up there rumbling through my stuff.

Even though I was mad at him, I couldn't lie. I needed him to make love, fuck, do *something* to me ASAP. I had been going out of my mind waiting for him to come back. Ever since the day I met him, I had not physically slept with anyone else, and I was proud of it. Usually, he did an awesome job, and I needed a refresher package.

Hopefully, I was not the only one burning with a desire to make love. Hopefully, James wanted me as much as I wanted him.

"Baby, can't you turn down that air conditioner...just a little bit?" James yelled down the stairs.

Chuckling to myself, I stood up and headed to the control box.

"Anything for you, sweetness," I called up to him and turned the temperature down a few. His job had him quarantining alone, but damn! What about me?

"What is that smell, Christine?! I thought you said the cat was gone? You got to start doing better, man, especially with this virus shit going around. What happened to the cleaning supplies I left here the last time?" James' voice was full of irritation and anger. He was totally killing the mood I was in.

I did put the cat out the last time he was here, but hell! He and Harper were both gone, and I hated being alone. Tyri was my only friend right now. When he came back, I sure did let him back in.

Suddenly, James came down the stairs with a full duffel bag. His masculine frame was so inviting, but his face said something totally different.

If he would have called me and said that he was coming by, I would have made sure that the house was somewhat presentable, but he didn't. He just showed up – unannounced and mad. This was some bullshit.

I rushed over to him, unbuttoning my skin-tight jeans. I wanted to show him that I meant business. My body was amazing. I had a petite structure with large breasts and apricot skin that I had covered with a green tube top. My blonde hair was pulled back in a tight ponytail to keep my hair out of my face. I struck a seductive pose and smiled at him.

"Damn, James," I said in a whiny voice. "You don't miss me?" I impatiently waited him for him to respond, exposing my breasts. "C'mon, baby. Why are

17

you just standing there? I can't wait. I missed you so much. I know you miss me?"

Usually, that line worked on James like a charm, but this time, it didn't. The look on his face was one that I was not too familiar with.

"When was the last time you washed your ass, Chris?" he asked. "I can *smell* you. Clean up this house and take a shower. You know, the house has to be decent for Harper to come home. When is she coming home?"

Damn, I knew I wasn't fresh, but did he have to call me out like that? I had been depressed with all the shit going on. The only things I had to comfort me were my cigarettes and some Boone's Farm wine. It had been years since I used drugs, but my skin told a different story.

What was J suppose to do?

It had been months since I had last seen Harper, and she only called once a week to check on my daddy. Even in Juvie, Harper's voice was strong and didn't need me. She owed James and me an apology for stabbing him, but he had the nerve to be worried about her coming home? She lied on him and to the people! Hell naw, she was not coming back here until she changed her story. I needed the money that James gave me for this house and could not afford to lose that to anyone, especially not my child!

"I don't know when she is coming home," I told him. "Her court date was put on hold with everything transitioning to virtual. I think her ass needs to sit in there anyway though. Her anger issues have to get under control, and I need them to give me a bigger check for having to deal with her craziness!"

I rubbed my hand on his chest, trying to turn his attention back to me.

"Come get in the shower with me, baby," I said. "Come wash me."

I looked up into his smoky, hazel eyes and smiled. This man was so damn fine, a Michael Ealy look-alike with light brown skin and beautiful eyes.

"Naw, man! I am about to go," he said. "I only stopped by to get some more of my shit. How am I more worried about your child than you are? Get your shit together, Chris, and get your baby home. Don't call me again until you have an update on Harper, okay?"

Not waiting for me to respond, he pushed passed me and opened the door. I couldn't believe this shit. Harper was all he cared about. *What about me?*

As the door closed behind him, I went back to the couch and relit the cigarette I was smoking. *Yeah, I*

What was I suppose to do?

will clean up, I thought, but *after I get my nerves together*.

From the pen of: *Nicola*

Harper

It had been a week since the Girls Who Brunch was here, and I was still smiling. The leader, Ms. Ni'cola, I swear, I just love her. The event was SO GOOD! The other speakers answered our questions one by one. Some were even crying from being so open and vulnerable, telling us all of their secrets and giving advice on how we could be better.

I am not going to lie. I have been to so many "empowerment" events, where the women tell us they are just like Beyoncé and woke up like this. They talked down to us, but this event was so different.

The DJ was a female DJ on the radio here in Vegas, who I had seen on so many flyers on Instagram, and she was right there in Juvie with us. Everyone was so dope. Another lady brought food and supplies for us all the way from D.C.

We can't get our stuff until we are released from custody, but just knowing that the stuff was there for us when we left here was a great feeling. My mamma hadn't even brought me anything or came to visit me. This lady, who was an absolute stranger, made sure that all of this was done for us. I would never forget her.

That's how I was feeling when I was called down to Visitation and found out it was Ms. Ni'cola. I sat down across from her at the table, shocked. I thought she said she lived in Atlanta. Why was she still here?

"Peace, Queen!" she said softly, smiling at me.

"How are you doing?"

The way she said "Peace, Queen!" was so powerful! When I heard it, it just made me light up and I felt like I was really a queen. I sat up straighter and responded in my best voice, "Peace, Queen," I said back to her.

"I brought you some hand sanitizers and gloves. I know it is not the cleanliest in here, and with this virus going around, you can't be too careful. I planned to stay here for two weeks, but I am leaving tomorrow to make sure I can get back home before anything else happens. But, before I left, I wanted to drop off a bunch of hygiene stuff to you. You are going to need it when you go home," she said.

Even though I didn't know when I was going home, I did appreciate her thinking of me.

"So, Harper," she continued, "the real reason why I am here is because I wanted to give you some good news. I saw the look on your face when I mentioned you going home, but I am serious. You will be going home today – well, not home, but at least to your aunt's house."

She stopped talking to see my reaction, but I didn't have one. I had heard the words that were coming out of her mouth, but my mind was not comprehending what she was saying exactly. I sat frozen in my seat. I couldn't move, let alone blink. I was just trying to take it all in. The only aunt I had was my Great Aunt Laura, and she was not too fond of me. My grandmother passed away before I was born and Aunt Laura was her sister. She lived in Pahrump, a little country city a few hours away from here.

I wasn't sure if it was because I was half-black, or because of the situation that led to me being born, but something made this woman dislike me. She would often say, "You are pretty for one of those mulatto girls, but you are going to have a hell of a time finding a good man to be your husband."

Why did she wish bad on me?

I would tell myself that she was mean to me because of her beef with my mamma and my upbringing to keep me from hating her. Or, maybe it was because of my relationship with my papa. Whatever the reason was, it made it even harder to believe that she had agreed to have me come home to her. But at that time, I was happy with anything.

"After you confided in me that you were pregnant," Ni'cola said, "there was no way I could live with myself if I left you here. I know firsthand how it feels to be pregnant as a teen, but I also know for a fact that I wouldn't have been able to do it in a place like this. I spoke to Officer Mead and your social worker, Ms. Manuel. They both agreed that this was not the best place for a baby, especially with all that is going on in the world. You need to be safe and at home – not behind bars."

Still in a daze, my head started to spin. *Damn!* Hearing those words spoken out loud made things so final to me, and I hated thinking about it.

Yes, I am pregnant, but I had been trying to pretend that I wasn't. On top of all the other shit that I had going on, worrying about a baby was not at the top of my list of priorities. *Hmmm, maybe that is why Aunt Laura was taking me in? She felt sorry for this baby, like she felt sorry for me?*

I found out I was pregnant a few days before I got here. Besides James, I had never had sex before, and my period was very inconsistent. So, my period being delayed didn't spark any concern, but I knew something was wrong. I couldn't stop throwing up. The feeling was so bad and I felt so weak that I took an uber to Smith's Food King on Civic Center and picked up a test.

Sitting on that toilet in their bathroom felt like an eternity, but it did not take long for the test to read positive. I was really pregnant by that fool. All the while, my mamma acted like that dude was so amazing.

Yea, I knew the story of how he saved her ass from the streets. A modern-day superhero. He met her for a "date," found out she was a mother, and wanted to protect us. He bought us from her pimp and the rest was history. Yes, you heard me right. My mamma had a pimp and was on crystal meth for a long time. Her face told the story. Even though she was only thirty-three years old, the drugs had made her facial features look almost like Skeletor from Star Wars. If Papa didn't have all those pictures of her before she was on drugs, I would have never known how much I looked like her. My mother was beautiful, but life kicked her ass horribly.

James did help get her clean. He helped her get public assistance, an apartment, and now, he was our family. She even tried to make me call him Daddy James, but Papa always advised me not to do it.

"When you start giving people titles that they truly did not earn, it sets you up for a world of trouble in the future, you hear me?" I remember Papa saying. "That man is James and if he or your mamma have a problem with it, you have them call me, okay?"

That is what sparked all the rage inside of me to stab James. It was already bad enough that that fool had the audacity to come back and forth into the house after doing this to me, acting like nothing happened, but now, I had a piece of him growing inside of me? That was going too far, especially because my mamma had wanted so badly to give him a baby. In her head, she thought that was going to make him move in full-time, but I had heard her say on the phone to her friend that he was always "too careful."

So, if this dude was so great with protection, why did he not only rape me, but didn't even have the courtesy to wear a condom?

That shit blew my mind every time I thought about it. I thought I could keep it a secret, but once they book you, each inmate must see a nurse and get a complete physical. Since I hadn't had my cycle, they made me pee on a stick.

When my social worker, Ms. Manuel, came to speak to me, she asked if I knew I was pregnant. At first, I tried to appear devastated, but the look in my eyes told on me.

"Harper, I need you to be honest with me, okay?" she said. "Is that the reason you stabbed your step-father? Is he the father of your child?"

She asked me this question with so much concern in her voice that I wanted to believe she cared about me. I nodded, yes, and stared at the wall. The situation was horrible, but what else was there for me to do? At least I knew who my baby daddy was. A lot of girls my age didn't even know that. Hell, my mamma didn't know who my daddy was. I guess I was a step ahead of the people – fucked up situation or not.

Outside of the staff, I did not feel comfortable telling anyone what was going on with me. At least if I could keep it a secret, I wouldn't have to worry about anyone trying to hurt my baby. Although I really hadn't been eating, the bulge in my stomach was growing every day. The hospital scrub type of top I wore helped to hide my secret, but for how long?

So, when Ms. Ni'cola came over to speak to me in private, the words, "I'm pregnant" just blurted out. Even though she could not physically touch me, the look in her eyes confirmed that hugging me was all she wanted to do.

I told her the entire story – about how James, my mamma's long-term boyfriend, raped me and tried to pretend like it didn't happen. I told her about how I had to go day in and day out in that crazy ass house, watching my mamma kiss his ass. The whole time his child grew inside of me. I told her about how once I found out that I was pregnant, I stabbed him, and my mamma still stood by his side, saying fuck me.

I didn't want to even look at her because I knew she was going to be disgusted by all this crazy information. However, by the look on Ms. Ni'cola's face, she felt just the opposite, and I knew that she took me seriously. Her reaction was the way I would assume a mother's would be if she found out about her daughter, not putting her man first, like my mother had. This woman was a Godsend.

It blew my mind to know that she was working on my situation before she left Vegas. No one ever cared about me like that. The tears just ran down my face as I sat across from her, and I could help but smile. It sucked that it wasn't my mamma fighting to get me out, but at least I was going home.

34

James

"Nevada governor extends COVID-19 shutdown until end of April, urges residents to shelter-in-place," said the news reporter.

What the fuck! Another month of this shit?

I have never been into the news before, but since this pandemic happened, I seem to have a sudden fascination with News 13 and everything that they have to say on the subject of this weird ass shit, COVID-19.

"Gov. Steve Sisolak has extended all of the state's emergency actions to mitigate spread of COVID-

19 — including closure of public and private schools, a nonessential business shutdown and ban on large gatherings — until the end of April, while urging state residents to shelter in place.

The governor's updated order, released by his office on Wednesday morning, is the latest signal by state authorities that the massive disruptions to normal public life needed to combat the spread of the virus are nowhere near over yet.

Although the initial length of the school closures and nonessential businesses shutdown were set to expire in mid-April, the governor said extending the closures, which includes casinos, was a necessary public health step. The new emergency directive, however, does not include penalties for those who don't comply."

I put the TV on silent, shaking my head, and looked out the window.

I didn't know how much longer I could keep up with this game of charades I had invented. I needed to come up with a plan if I was going to come out of this on the winning side.

"Baby. Why did you mute the news? I wanted to hear what the new plans are," Yolanda said, emerging from the kitchen.

She had Junior perched on her hip, fighting him to release her reddish-brown tresses, which my son inherited. The same color as Harper's hair.

Yalonda was the perfect package. Beautiful, smart, submissive, and most of all, in love with me. She was a realtor and set us up nicely with so many corporate investment properties, that we were actually doing pretty well – even through the shutdown. I could

From the pen of: _Nicra_

not afford to lose her, but if I didn't get this shit together, I knew for a fact she was not going to continue to take my bullshit.

"My bad, love," I said. "I am just over hearing about the coronavirus. I think I am starting to have anxiety about it." I said, pointing the remote back in the direction of the TV and pressing the unmute button.

"Thanks, babe," my wife replied. "I am almost done with lunch and then, I am going to take the baby for a walk. Do you want something from out of here?"

I shook my head, no. Yolanda smiled at me and retreated to the kitchen.

"In total, the order extends a slew of emergency directives issued by Sisolak over the last two weeks that have upended public life in the state, drastic measures deemed necessary by medical professionals to slow the spread of the virus. These include..."

I tuned out the news and pulled out my vape. I sat back in my recliner and took a long drag. I needed to calm my nerves and quick.

Yolanda was going to kill me, leave me, or both if she only knew all the shit that had transpired over the past few months. From the shit that happened between Harper and I, that it was really Harper who had stabbed me, and the fact that Harper was Christine's daughter was enough for the history books.

You see, the shit is complicated.

I met Christine some years back when Yolanda and I were at a crossroads in our relationship. We were finally pregnant, and during her sixth month, she had a miscarriage with our first son. It was bad enough that his heart stopped, but she had to still deliver him. An hour and a half later, my first son, Isaiah, was born, but he never took his first breath.

For hours, my wife sat there, cradling him. She didn't say a word to me or anyone else that came into the room to pay their respects to us. She just focused on Isaiah. That's it. From that moment on, for the next few months, I lost my wife. Literally. She wouldn't work, eat, or even leave his nursery.

"Yolanda is experiencing postpartum depression and grieving at the same time," Dr. Chow informed me over the phone. My wife had just missed her six-week checkup. "Just give her some time. She will come out of it," the doctor reassured me.

I heard him, but what was I supposed to do until she came back? That shit was hurting me as well, but nobody seemed to care how I felt. Everyone just cared about my wife's feelings. I got it, but hell. That was my first born as well. My heart was broken, but I guess I was the man so I was supposed to just deal with it.

What was I suppose to do?

It had been weeks since my wife had even touched me, let alone had sex with me. A brother was in need. I was longing to feel some kind of affection. I worked in personal security for some local celebrities in Las Vegas, and I worked as a bouncer for a few clubs. I was always telling out-of-towners how to get a girl for the night.

"Just go to www.LasVegasDirect.com, search 'finding sex in Las Vegas,' and boom. A list of girls in every price range, evert demographic, and every nationality," I would often tell them. From the responses I got at the club the next night, the listing actually worked.

That is where I met Christine. Like I said, I was desperate. I wanted something totally different and way more extreme. Now, I thought, *how am I going to keep all of this shit together? Especially now that we were in the middle of a crazy ass pandemic?*

I unmuted the TV and changed the channel. Since all the sports were cancelled, I had to watch some reality television reruns. Anything to clear my mind from all of this bullshit

Five years before….

Christine

*M*amma I am hungry and there is no food in the house. Mamma, wake up!"

I opened my eye a crack and moaned. I had a long night, and this girl was really blowing my high. My ten-year-old daughter stood over me with her hands resting on both of her hips.

"Damn, girl! Be quiet, shit!" I snapped at Harper. Sometimes, I thought that girl forgot that I was the mamma and she was the kid. I had to admit it, my baby was really responsible and helpful, but right now, I was not in the mood to put up with her shenanigans.

I rolled over onto my stomach and rubbed the sleep out of my eyes. I just barely fell asleep and here this child comes, demanding me to get up! What I wouldn't give for a chance to sleep in on a Saturday morning, like the folks on TV.

"Mamma, I am sorry for interrupting your sleep, but the water is not working," Harper said, not sounding too empathetic. "I can't do my chores and there ain't no food in the fridge. I was gonna make us breakfast, but I couldn't. Can you please go to the store or give me some money? I will go to the store myself."

Harper transferred her body weight from the left to the right, all while staring me down. I guess I was taking too long to respond, so the child had the nerve to roll her eyes at me. I was about to slap the shit out of

Harper, but then realized why my daughter was jumping bad with me.

The cover slipped off of me, and I only had on my bra with a thong. I pulled the blanket back over me and ordered her to get out. "Give me a minute to get dressed," I said, "and I'll run to the store real quick. Okay?" Harper nodded her head and stormed out in disgust, slamming the door behind her. I shook my head and rolled back over in the bed. After a while, I finally got up and slipped into my night shirt.

When James called to tell me he was outside, I'm sure he didn't need me to get completely naked this morning. Apparently, he had just gotten back into town and was on his way to get some rest. He was craving some of my peach sweetness and informed me of that when I opened the door, letting him in.

I barely pulled my night shirt over my head before he started opening a pack of Magnum condoms with his teeth. He pulled his dick out of his pants and commanded me to suck it. I dropped to my knees and tenderly took his dick in my mouth. He pulled my titties out of the bra. He fondled my swelling breast with his hands, as he violently pumped his dick in my mouth. He damn near caused me to choke.

I missed James so much. I actually asked him to stop by on his way home, but I did not know he was about to treat me like a $5 hoe who worked the streets. He was the one who reminded me that I didn't need to work on the streets, but whenever he treated me like this, it made me have my doubts. In one swift motion, he turned me over onto all fours. James slapped that condom onto his Johnson and let loose into me.

At first, he pushed my thong to the side, but then complained that the material rubbed against his dick too harshly, James told me to take it off. After a couple more pumps, I felt James tense up inside of me. He dug his nails into my hips, meaning that he was about to climax.

Once he reached his ecstasy, James wobbled into the bathroom with his pants pushed midway down his thighs. Disgusted, I got into the bed, pouting. *I didn't even cum, shit!* I thought that after I broke down to him how much I missed him, he would dedicate some real time to me. Look at how wrong I was. James came out of the bathroom and finally decided to ask me how I was doing.

"Baby, come lay with me for a minute?" I asked him, but I already knew the answer.

"Girl, you know I have to hurry and go home," he said. "I just stopped by here real quick because I know I have a bunch of shit to do tomorrow, and I didn't want to hear your mouth."

Seeing the disappointment on my face, James promised that he was going to come back if he was done with everything early. He peeled off $500 from the stack in his pocket and gave it to me. James kissed me roughly on the cheek and hurried out the door.

Glancing at the clock, I saw it was 3:36. Wow, a new world record. James's visit had only lasted a total of 18 minutes. I was mad as hell, but really didn't know why. That shit was typical for the men I was used to.

I got out of bed and made sure the door was locked. We had just moved into this apartment a few months ago, and I was still nervous about the neighborhood. We were living in a daily-weekly, which was a step higher than a motel. I had been on the Section 8 list for some time now and had to settle for a public housing apartment (also known as the projects.)

Originally, I'm from Pahrump, a city famous for all of its brothels and barbecue. It's sad to say, but I was a product of both. My daddy used to make the best barbecue in the city and sold dinner plates every day to all the brothels. Brothels are legal locations where men can visit prostitutes. Even though my daddy should have protected me from the brothels of Pahrump and everything about them, as soon as I was old enough to drive, I became a delivery girl. Brothels, like the Chicken Ranch, made my family so much money that my daddy didn't care. I know that to this day, it's one of his biggest regrets when it comes to me.

Back then, I didn't know exactly what a brothel was. The only thing I did know was that the women who worked in there were so beautiful and dressed in clothes that I had only seen on T.V. I used to go back home and tell my daddy all about them. He would tell me not to pay them any mind and send me out on my next delivery. I love my daddy, but now I know, he should've talked to me about what was going on at those brothels. Really, he should have kept me away from them altogether.

It didn't take long before I was recruited to work at one of the brothels and the rest of was history. At first, it was fun to play dress up with the other girls. I didn't know how to do my own makeup, so they had artists on-site to make me beautiful. The men we serviced were called "johns." Most of the johns who visited the brothel I worked at were older. They just wanted to watch me walk around and fondled me a bit. It took a few months before I had my first real sexual experience, and I hated it. The man was full of libations, which isn't uncommon. In fact, he was just like the rest of the johns I had seen before, but it didn't make him tired and goofy. This man was aggressive and it damn near felt like rape.

I didn't think it was going to be like that, and it made me want to leave. Our house mother, Lynn, gave me some pills to soothe my nerves, and my life went downhill from there. I became dependent on the pills. Before I knew it, I kept needing stronger and stronger fixes until the day that one of my regulars, Carlos, introduced me to crystal meth. Carlos was fine as hell! He was of Columbian decent and had the prettiest dark eyes. His solid build and chisel chest did something to me, and I really started to believe this guy was my man.

Carlos visited me regularly for a few months before he convinced me that I could make triple the money in Vegas. The town was bigger and brighter, and until I got on my feet, he would even let me come live with him. I thought that was the best thing in the world that anyone could do for me, but I was so DAMN WRONG!

He did help me, but not in the way I thought he would. He became my pimp, and I was his hoe. In the beginning, he would at least have sex with me, but that soon faded away. I was only allowed to sleep on the floor in the living room and only if I met the quota he gave me for the day. If not, he left me outside to work until I met my goal. He would often say, "Shit, Christine! You're a snow bunny. Those tricks love bitches with blonde hair and blue eyes! You must not be working hard enough. Pay attention and get it together."

Every day, I worked hard trying to prove myself to Carlos, but nothing was ever good enough. I think I worked too hard because not long after that, I became pregnant. I didn't know who the father was because I serviced 10-15 men a night on a bad day.

When I found out I was pregnant, I didn't want an abortion. In fact, learning the news made me want the total opposite. I wanted to keep it. I wanted love from something or someone. I wanted to have something that belonged to me. I tried to hide it from Carlos, but it didn't take long for him to figure it out. He knew he wasn't spending money on my Tampax bill anymore. When he made the connection, he assured me that the monkey inside of my belly was not going to stop the show.

Actually, it meant that I had to work that much harder because we were going to have another mouth

53

to feed, and that is what I did. I worked so hard that I got picked up for prostitution during my eighth month of pregnancy and had to sit in jail to clear up all of my warrants.

At the time, I thought giving birth in jail was the worst thing that could have happened to me, but it turned out to be the best. My labor with Harper wasn't long, and even though I had been doing terrible things to my body, my baby came out strong and stubborn. Harper possessed a head of dark red curls. Her skin was rose colored and she had green eyes. She was beautiful, like one of the models in the magazines I read, so I named my baby, Harper Collins. Since I had been off of drugs for those few months in jail, I was able to think clearly. I knew that I didn't want my baby to end up in the system, but I definitely didn't want her to end up in Carlos's arms.

I was able to hold my baby for a few hours before the guard told me that my father and aunt were here to pick up my baby. *OH MY GOD!* I was so relieved. My baby was going to be safe! But that's how Harper ended up in Pahrump. I didn't get her back until last year when my Daddy got sick. Soon after, I met James and he rescued us.

I finally got out of the bed and went in the bathroom. I looked at myself in the mirror and pushed my hair out of my face. Back in the day, some people would have considered me beautiful, but now, I knew I needed work. My body was my best asset and I didn't even have one stretch mark. I was thick in all of the right places and stood almost five feet tall. Even though my body was so bomb, I couldn't make a man stick around. That was why James was so different. I needed to make him fall in love with me. I needed to give him a family.

Oh well. I shrugged my shoulders. Can't cry over spilled milk. At least I got some money behind it. And boy, did I need it to get the water back on. I brushed my hair into a lazy ponytail. I decided to get dressed and go do what Princess Harper had commanded. I pulled on a pair of jean shorts and a yellow tank top, then slid on my flip-flops.

"Harper!" I called. "I am about to go get some food and pay a few bills. Is there anything else you need? Because when I come back, I want to sleep. You hear me?"

"No, Mamma," Harper said in a sweet and innocent voice.

"Okay, baby. I'll get you some chips too, okay?" I said.

I knew that would bring a smile to any child's face, even Harper's, and I was right.

"Lock the door, and don't let anyone in unless it is James, okay? I love you."

I walked outside and heard the locks on the door click behind me. I started the long trek down the stairs to the parking lot. We were on the third floor, so I was ecstatic that my baby did not have a long grocery list. I hated lugging all of those bags up to the top floor. As I walked to my car, all eyes were on me, so I gave a show. I swayed the fullness of my hips with every step. Men watched me, but didn't wish I was their girl. They watched me because they wanted to sleep with me. Women always turned up their noses when they saw me, like they just knew what I used to be.

Once I was inside of my car, I did my daily routine. I closed my eyes and said a short prayer for the car to start. When I opened my eyes, I turned the key in the ignition. I heard it hesitate, but it started. *Thank you, Jesus!* I put it in reverse and began my journey to the store.

I was at the light on Carey when a white Range Rover pulled up beside me. It was Carlos, my old pimp, but he was in the passenger seat. He was nodding his head to the music when he glanced over in my direction and smiled at me.

I didn't smile back. Anxiously, I waited for the light to change and sped off. I didn't go to the store. I had to make sure that the duo wasn't following me. Once I saw them turn left onto Civic Center, I finally let out a deep breath. I was trying so hard to stay clean and stay away from my past life. I was trying to have my family with James. I had to make this work, man. I had to be able to have my family.

Harper

"Aunt Laura, are you awake?" I whispered softly outside her door.

It was close to midnight, but I needed my aunt to wake up. I had just entered my ninth month of pregnancy, and I was feeling so uncomfortable. This baby was doing all kinds of flips and turns inside of me. I had been lying in bed for hours in so much pain.

"What is it? It's late, Harper. Are you feeling okay?" Aunt Laura's shrill voice called out from behind the door.

Before I woke up my aunt, I called Ms. Ni'cola first. She urged me to have my aunt take me to the hospital. I knew it was 3 a.m. in Atlanta, but she told me to call her if I needed anything. Since my release from jail, Ms. Ni'cola had been paying for me to ride Ubers to and from my doctor appointments and helped me all the way through this process.

"I – I think I am in labor," I answered.

Through the door I could hear my shuffling around.

"Are you sure? Give me a minute," Said my aunt.

I leaned against the wall and took in some deep breaths.

"Yes, ma'am," I replied. "Ms. Ni'cola told me not to wake you unless my contractions were coming closer together. Right now, they are about four minutes apart. Aunt Laura, I am scared. Can you please call the paramedics?" It didn't make sense for her to take me to the hospital. With COVID-19 procedures, I knew they wouldn't even allow my family into the delivery room. "Can you please hold my hand, Aunt Laura?" I asked. "I am so scared."

I heard her on the phone, giving the 9-1-1 operator our address and my information.

Even though the shutdown had ended, Covid-19 was still real, and everyone was being so careful. I was scared about going to the hospital alone to deliver, but I didn't want to put my aunt at risk, especially after she had been so kind to me and took me in. A few weeks after moving in with her, I found out that she had lung cancer. She was at a higher risk to complications if she got sick, and I would have gone crazy if I was the cause of anything happening to her.

"Shh, Shh, Shh! You are going to be okay," Aunt Laura tried to reassure me. She pulled up a chair so I can sit. I took a few deep breaths in and slowly blew out trying to catch my breath.

I knew it sounded crazy, but I wanted my mom. The last time I had spoken to her was the day I was released from Juvie. My aunt was fussing at her on the phone, ripping her a new one!

"This child is getting ready to have a baby," she had said, "and you don't have the decency to come and see about her? You are her mother, and she needs you!"

I didn't know exactly what my mother had said to my aunt, but my Aunt Laura abruptly handed me the phone.

"Hello?" I said meekly into the phone.

"Why the FUCK WOULD YOU TELL AUNT LAURA THAT JAMES WAS YOUR

MOTHERFUCKING BABY DADDY?" my mother's screamed at me. "HE IS ALL THAT WE GOT, HARPER, AND YOU ARE TRYING TO TAKE HIM AWAY FROM ME?"

Over the years, I had listened to my mother scream and holler at me about everything. Nothing I did was good enough. I hated that lady with all my might and loved her at the same damn time. What the hell was wrong with me?

She either took me away from the people that I loved, or she allowed the ones that she loved to do anything to me. When my papa was sick, my mamma and Uncle Carlos came to get me. I was only nine years old when he started running his fingers between the soft spot between my legs while my mother was out working. I remember the first time he did it. "I can't wait until you are all the way ripe," he whispered into my ear. "I am going to have so much fun with you."

I told my mom and she blamed it on me.

"If he did it, it's because you are frolicking around here being fast," she said. "Blinking your eyes at him and shit. Don't fuck this up for me, Harper. He was good to us and took us in. Do not fuck this up for us."

So, I started staying after school and helping my teachers for as long as I could. I would get home at about 5 p.m., and then I would lock myself in the bathroom, pretending that I was sick. I did this every day until James bought us from Uncle Carlos.

Now, my mother was doing the same thing with James. I was tired of it. I wished she was not my mamma anymore! We were in the middle of a deadly pandemic. Folks were dropping dead like flies, and the only thing she cared about was James.

I couldn't take it anymore. I listened to this lady scream and holler. Once she stopped, I took a deep breath and said slowly, "You are a terrible mother, and you are dead to me. You will never see me or my baby girl. You are fucking dead to me."

I threw the phone on the couch and cried, trying to calm down. This was my first pregnancy, and according to Dr. Kenny, I was healthy. I had not had any complications, but I had officially reached the uncomfortable stage of my pregnancy. I have done everything I could do to protect my baby, and once I found out I was having a girl, I promised her that I was never going to be anything like my mamma.

Aunt Laura came over and rubbed my head.

"Shh, shh. Do not cry, child. My sister is turning over in her grave knowing that her daughter is acting like this," she said. "I used to be so hard on you because I didn't want you to end up like your mother. Your papa spoiled her and let her get her away with everything. The repercussions from that is biting us all in the butt now."

That was the first time my aunt had spoken to me without barking. She told me stories about my grandmother, papa, and my mom. I learned more about her and why she was alone. That was the first time I felt that she could really see me. After that, our relationship changed, and I finally found myself happy there with her.

Now, it's time for me to have this child and the only person that I wanted was my mother. Was that disrespectful to my aunt? To Ms. Ni'cola?

What was I suppose to do?

I guess Aunt Laura had read my mind. As she rubbed my head. "It's okay to love your mom, baby. She is the only mother you have, baby. She is the only mother that you have," she said, rubbing my head.

We could hear the sirens coming closer. Aunt Laura kissed me on the forehead and got up to open the door.

From the pen of: *Nicola*

James

When I thought to myself as I hung up on Christine, fuming from my ears.

She had been doing this shit for a long time, but damn, Harper was only fifteen years old. How long are you going to try to make me her daddy, but you aren't her mother? Her fucked up thought process and dumb ass tactics were why I didn't want to be with her. Naw, let me keep it real with myself first. I was only around because I wanted to protect Harper. She looked like my wife was her birth mother, and I wanted to protect her.

I remember the night I met Christine. I saw a picture of Harper on her cellphone screensaver. I remember asking her, "Is she yours?"

"Yes, she is my heart," Christine replied.

How was it possible for a smoked-out person like Christine to produce a doll baby like that? Harper and my wife both possessed the same reddish brown tresses and reddish skin tone. Instantly, I wanted to protect Harper. Yalonda and I had lost so many babies, and I could financially care for all of them, but this person who was selling her ass for money had been blessed with a child?

Just how that seemed crazy, what I did next was even more bonkers. That night, I never slept with Christine. I just talked to her about changing her life. I took her back home to her pimp, asked him the price for both of them, and I paid $2000 for Christine and

$3000 for Harper. That fool even had the audacity to try and sell me the baby by herself. He told me how sweet she was going to be. Less than thirty minutes later, I had both of them in my truck, and now, I was literally a surrogate father for both of them!

Christine just called to let me know that Harper was in labor. She was heated that Harper was still accusing me of being the daddy.

I got up off the couch and went to check on my family. They were both fast asleep in the bed. Yalonda was lying on her back while Junior was snuggled up in the crook of her arm.

I wondered what would happen if she found out I was about to have another baby with a child – if she would leave me and take my son.

I felt sorry for Harper, and to add insult to injury, I took that poor baby's innocence. And I know for a fact that I did because there was blood all over me in the morning.

She had to grow up so fast because her mother was trying to find herself. How I felt about it was plain and simple. If you haven't found yourself by now, then damn! You're never going to. When I got to the house, Harper was in the kitchen, making TikTok videos. Sometimes, I would watch in awe how Harper could just sit on her phone for hours, creating and editing her videos with ease.

I looked around to see if Christine was home. It wasn't weird for Harper to be home for hours, but it *was* unusual for Christine not to be blowing up my phone. She made it so difficult to keep up this façade I was playing to balance her place and home. I was getting tired of having to constantly lie about being out of town on business trips every week. It felt like I was supposed to be out of town every week.

I picked up the phone and called her. It only rang once and went straight to voicemail.

"Hey babe. Where are you?" I asked. "I am going to chill here with Harper until you get back. Wanted to drop off some money to you."

Christine entered the house, struggling, as I pushed the end button on my phone.

"I brought dinner," she said, smiling. She was carrying several McDonald's bags.

I rolled my eyes and sat down on the couch. Christine thought she was slick, but I wasn't going to let her get away with this so easily. I was not in the mood to talk. I was too frustrated and wanted to stop having a double life. Part of me wanted to say, "Fuck

73

it," and take Harper home with me. The crazy thing is how well Harper's temperament and physical looks blended with my real family. Maybe God brought me into this situation for just that.

"Christine. I can't keep doing this with you," I said, trying to pick a fight. I didn't want to stay long, and I hoped a fight would do me some justice.

"You can't keep doing what with me?" Christine asked, flipping that ponytail of hers and plopping down onto the couch. "Harper! Go run and get my weed box. I had a long day and coming home to all this fussing is giving me a headache. I need to roll up!"

Harper got up and slammed her phone down on the table. She hated being disturbed while she filming on that phone.

"Girl! Do you have an attitude?" Christine asked.

I don't know why or how Harper got under Christina's skin the way that she did. It seemed like she got pleasure out of yelling and fighting with her daughter. "Fuck that phone! I just pawned my iPad to pay the phone bill, and that is how you are gonna act when I tell you to do something?" she yelled. Christina rushed into the kitchen and got into Harper's face.

Harper crossed her arms in front of her body and didn't respond. She glared back at her, looking her square in the eyes. It was as if she was silently letting her know that she was not afraid of her.

The two women stood there for a few seconds staring each other down before Christine pushed Harper into the wall.

"What? You want to hit me, Harper? You think you bad and want to hit me? I will fuck you up! Do you hear me? I don't have to deal with this. I can send your red ass up out of here. Hit me, Harper. I dare you!"

Christine was screaming at the top of lungs. Her face turned beet red.

Harper just glared at her, not speaking. She pushed past Christine and stomped up the stairs, slamming the door to her room. As mad as her mother made her, Harper never responded to the madness verbally, but her silent responses were powerful statement pieces.

I don't know if Christina was madder at Harper's slamming or if it was because the young girl was unfazed by her antics, but Christine was pissed.

I have witnessed Christine slapping Harper, pushing her, and punching her over little to nothing. Everything that child did was a trigger for Christine. According to her, Harper was the worst kid alive. She would bellow that from the mountain tops, letting anyone who would listen know how horrible her daughter was. She even warned me to be careful around Harper because she liked lying on men, saying they touched her.

What kind of mother says things like that?

That the reason why I put up with Christine is because I needed to be around to protect Harper as much as I could.

I could see the rage built up in Christine's face as she was about to chase after Harper. I wanted to snap, but instead, I did something totally different than what I usually do. I am still live with the regret of that decision today.

"Christine, go get the weed and let's smoke," I said.

When I said those words, her mood instantly changed. I had never smoked weed with her before. Hell, I never smoke. I wasn't that dude, but I needed to do something to change the mood in that house.

Like a kid in a candy store, Christine's frown instantly turned into a smile. She hurried up and grabbed the box off of the top of the refrigerator. I walked into the kitchen and grabbed a hamburger from the bag. I hoped that if I ate something, it would ease the intensity of the high.

Christine sat at the table, watching my every move. She had never seen me high before and probably didn't know what to do next. I did get Christine off of crystal meth, but I did compromise with her by allowing her to make weed her drug of choice. I hated drugs, but I think if popped one of the edibles, I should be okay.

"What kind of gummies do you have?" I asked, taking a bite into my burger.

Christine rummaged through her precious box and carefully pulled out a pack of gummies.

"Well, I was planning on rolling up, but since you are a new bootie, we can do edibles. Here, try this one," she responded.

I eyed the candy apprehensively. If this was going to keep her calm, then so be it.

Thank you," I said and popped the candy into my mouth.

At least it tastes good, I thought to myself.

Christine was so excited. She grinned from ear-to-ear. "See! It is not that bad," she said, popping a handful into her mouth. After a while, the floodgates of her mouth opened, and she started talking my ear off about everything.

I finished my burger and grabbed another gummy out of the bag.

"Harper, are you hungry?" I called out, but she didn't respond. Whenever they got into it like that, Harper usually disappeared and did not come back out. I hated this cycle, but what could I do? She was not my real daughter, but damn, I wished she was.

"Fuck Harper with her smart-ass mouth!" said Christine. "She thinks she's so grown, she can feed her damn self!"

Instantly frustrated, I popped two more edibles into my mouth.

Hell, this wasn't that bad, I thought to myself. I could have done this a long time ago. I ate a few more and tuned Christine out.

The room began to spin and my head started to hurt. Instantly, I was exhausted. I stood up, checking the time on my phone.

8:34! Oh my God! I was supposed to be home hours ago! I had four missed calls from Yolanda. I needed to take my ass home and try to sleep this shit off.

Standing up, I felt my knees wobble beneath me. I couldn't drive like this. Even though the couch was uncomfortable, I needed to lay down for a minute before I tried to go home.

"Come get into the bed!" Christine whined.

I would have preferred the bed, but at that moment, I knew I wasn't going to be able to make it.

"I- I am so-sorry, babe," I told her. "I got to go to work in the morning." "Let me just lay down real quick, and I have to go. But here." I pulled the money out of my pocket.

Seeing the money changed her pouty mood. She kissed me on the cheek and grabbed the money.

When she retreated the bedroom, I closed my eyes. I tried to mentally settle the queasy in my stomach. I took in a few deep breaths and everything suddenly went black.

When I heard the buttons of the microwave beep, I opened my eyes.

"Babe, what are you eating?" I asked when I saw my wife whisk past me.

No response.

"Pretty girl, come here," I called out.

My head felt like it was going to explode and I struggled to get up. I knew I had been fucking up lately and needed to get my shit together before I lost my family.

Holding onto the wall, I stumbled into the kitchen.

"Baby, are you ignoring me?" I asked.

Yolanda continued to ignore me. She stood at the microwave, reading something on her phone. I loved when she let her tresses flow, hanging down to almost her waist. The closer I got to her, I could smell the scent of shea butter. That clean scent turned me on so much that I even bought some for Christine to use when she got out of the shower.

I leaned in and wrapped my arms around her from behind, kissing the top of her head. Yolanda tensed up and didn't move.

"Baby, I am so sorry," I said. "I know I have been fucking up lately. Please forgive me. I am going to stop working so much. Please." I kissed the back of her neck and ran my hands down her hips.

She didn't say a word and still didn't move. Whenever she got upset, making love to her always changed her mood. She liked it when I took it, fucking her from behind.

I pulled my johnson out. I kneeled down and rubbed it against her ass. In one swift motion, I moved her panties to the side. I didn't give her an opportunity to say no. When I pushed myself into her, the more she tried to pull away from me, the more I took it.

I felt like I was moving in slow motion, but it went fairly quickly. She felt so tight and good, and she was so wet when I felt the precum release. "Damn baby,

you feel so damn good!" Exclaimed. Still, Yolanda
didn't say anything.

She loved it when I choked her, so I wrapped my
hands around her neck. Still Yolanda didn't respond
verbally.

Fuck, she is mad for real! I thought, but she
hadn't told me to stop, so I kept going.

I continued to penetrate her until I felt myself
release. It wasn't until I pulled out that I realized the
amount of blood down there.

"Baby, you're bleed –" I started and froze in my
tracks. It wasn't until then that I noticed how badly she
was shaking.

When I was trying to pull my pants up, Yalonda
finally said something.

W – wh – why did you do this to me?" she asked. "I thought you were different and loved me, like a daughter." It was Harper.

Hearing her voice fucked me up.

OH MY GOD – Harper. I just had sex with Harper! I opened my mouth, but no words came out. Crying, Harper ran out of the room.

That was the day I impregnated Harper. I really thought she was wife. I hated it when people blamed their indiscretions on being under the influence, but I was totally guilty of it!

I was the root of all the pain that Harper was feeling, and right now, she needed her mother. Today, I was going to make sure Christine was there for her.

I ran down the stairs and texted Christine: *I am on my way to get you so be ready. Stop hating your daughter and turn your anger on me. She was not lying you.*

I unlocked my car with my remote and hurried to get inside. I was scared of how Christine was going to react to my confession about violating her daughter, but enough was enough. I was tired of all of this SHIT!

I tossed my phone onto the passenger seat and started the car. Usually when I drove, I liked to bump some music, but I had so many thoughts and situations running through my head. I didn't touch the radio.

I pulled out of my subdivision and headed towards the expressway.

I wondered how Christine was going to treat Harper and the baby once she was delivered. I knew

From the pen of: *Nina*

that it was selfish of me to wonder, but I wanted to know what the baby's name was going to be.

As I waited on the arrow to change from red to green at the stoplight, I heard my phone notify me of a text message. It was a response from Christine.

I know she isn't lying. I saw what you did to her in the kitchen.

This bitch saw it and still turned against her daughter for me? I thought. *What kind of evil person is she?*

My heart was beating as intensely as I merged onto the freeway ramp. I was halfway through the intersection when an older Chevy Suburban came out of nowhere. It was charging full speed in my direction, head on. I tried to speed up and get out of its way, but I didn't move fast enough.

Before I knew it, our vehicles connected. My truck spun out of control. I tried to gain control of the steering wheel and turned it to the opposite direction, but my head was whipping from left to right, and my head hit the steering wheel.

"Lord!" I called out. "I am so sorry!" That was the last thing I said before everything went black for a second time.

From the pen of: *Nicola*

Christine

"What do you mean she at the hospital by herself?" I asked. "As much fussing and cussing you have been doing, I was sure that you were at least going to be there with Harper!" I was screaming into the phone.

My aunt didn't have any problem judging me or constantly reminding me how my lack of discipline was the reason why my life and my daughter were so fucked up.

From the pen of: *Nicha*

"I have cancer, Chris. I can't go to the hospital," my aunt whispered into the phone.

Cancer! Why didn't anyone tell me? I thought. I knew my life was fucked up, but I hated hearing about it. Since my brothel days, I had been living my life in a daze, either high or drunk off of something, and I hated it.

My aunt was dying and taking care of my pregnant daughter. I didn't even know how Harper got there. One day, she was in Juvie, and the next day, she wasn't. No one told me anything. I mean, I knew I haven't been Mother of the Year, chasing behind James, but I was still her mother.

"Your daughter is going to Desert View, if you care. She will be delivering your grandchild alone!" Aunt Laura said and hung up in my face.

What was I suppose to do?

I couldn't believe I had allowed this shit to spin out of control like this, but James was right about one thing. Harper did need me. Now, more than ever. For a long time, I thought James was brought into my life to save me, but after today, I had to stop pretending that I was weak. I needed to save myself and my child.

After Harper screamed at me, I laid alone on the couch and called James for empathy. Hell, I was doing all of this shit for him. I wanted to keep him in my life, but it was hard to hear him tell me how fucked up I was for not going. I thought I was showing everyone that we were a united front. It blew my damn mind.

I wiped the tears away from my eyes and sat up.

Girl! You are about to be a grandmother. Go to your daughter! I told myself.

I got into the shower to wash away the sour stench that lingered on skin from the lack of self-care the past few days. I had been in a funk, waiting on James to come over and trying not to think about Harper in Pahrump. I hated growing up there, and now, my baby was back there.

My reliance on James was the tool I used to make my daughter an enemy when I should have been protecting her.

While in the shower, I kept hearing my phone go off. I knew my aunt was upset, but after she hung up on me, I knew she was done fussing until the next big thing. So, it must have been James. It felt good to know he was staying stayed on me. It was the way I wanted my daddy to stay on me. He had allowed me to do any and everything I wanted, but when Harper came, he was always so protective of her.

How was that possible? How did a grandparent love his grandchild more than his only child?

The love my daddy gave Harper drove me crazy. So, in a way, when kept coming by, when he got me a place, a car, and he provided me with financial assistance, it was the most love I had ever gotten from any man my entire life.

I wrapped a towel around me and picked up the phone to read the messages.

I am on my way to get you so be ready. James texted. ***Stop hating your daughter and turn your anger on me. She was not lying you.***

Is he finally admitting what happened? I thought.

I had been compartmentalizing my feelings and pretending nothing happened, but I saw.

I saw him fondling her. Harper stood, frozen like a deer in headlights, with tears streaming down her face. My first reaction was to stop it, but he had just given us $500 and I needed it. I turned around and went back in my room, quietly closing the door. My heart was going so fast, but we needed him. Eventually, he was going to want her. She was beautiful.

The next morning, I saw the blood in my kitchen, and I knew how far things had gone. So, instead of going to my child, comforting her and protecting her, I made her the enemy.

I was over James talking to me condescendingly, like I was the only one with issues when he had skeletons too. Breathing heavily, I responded simply: ***I know she is not lying. I saw what you did to her in the kitchen.***

I dropped the phone, shaking.

It was the first time I said it out loud. How could he talk down to me while he was admitting that he fucked my kid!

I dropped my phone on the bed and hurried to get dressed.

Do I call the police on him? Will they try to press charges against me, too, for allowing it to happen?

We would have to address that problem once we got there. One problem at a time. Right now, I needed to be there for my daughter.

From the pen of: *Nicola*

Yalonda

"Who are you? What do you mean he was in an accident? Is he okay? Where is he?"

From a distance, I could hear the sirens and yelling in the background. It scared the hell out of me.

The officer took a deep breath and hesitated to respond.

"Ma'am, my name is Officer Patterson. Is your address: 2502 Dunbar Lane, Henderson, NV? We would like to speak to you in person, if that is okay?"

The officer's voice was very solemn and soft. I knew this call didn't mean anything good, but I was impatient.

"If you have my address already, why did you call? This has to be illegal, torturing someone like this. Can you please just tell me what the hell is going on?" I demanded.

I had finally gotten an appointment at the nail show, and I was waiting outside to enter. The baby was with my aunt, and I was excited. It was my first appointment since the pandemic had started, but now, I couldn't even think. "Where is my husband?" I asked.

I blinked a couple times. It felt like my vision was going blurry.

"I am so sorry. We found his registration in the glove compartment, but there was also a Nevada Power bill with an address in North Las Vegas, so I had to be sure. The accident took place in the 1000 block of Green Valley Pkwy. Your husband was entering the 215 when the accident took place. His phone was retrieved from the car by another officer. They were able to get into the device and located a contact called 'Wifey,' so I took the chance to call you."

"Thank you, Officer. I am on my way. Is James there? I am about 6 minutes away."

I sped up the street and prayed for James. I hoped he was okay.

From the pen of: *Nicola*

Three months later….

Harper

Morning, Laura!" I cooed at my baby. "Today is

mommy's birthday. Are you going to sing 'Happy

Birthday' to me, pretty girl? Are you going to give me a

party? Laura cooed back, kicking her legs and arms.

I wondered if my own mama hadn't been in jail

when she had me, would we have had an opportunity

to bond. Would we be closer?

For as long as I could remember, my papa was

all I had. He taught me everything I know. We went

fishing and hunting. When I was as young as four years old, he taught me how to use a knife to protect myself. His biggest fear was me growing up in Vegas. When I was nine, I was taken away from the only person who showed me unconditional love. That's why it was my duty to give my daughter the same love that my papa gave me.

Laura was literally my best friend. I think if Mamma had me, and not my papa, maybe our relationship would've been better. Laura was beautiful and my exact twin. She had the sweetest smile and was such a quiet baby. Mamma said she was just like me when I was little. I couldn't stop watching my baby. I still couldn't believe that she was mine. I named her Laura after my great-aunt. She took me in and showed me kindness when my own mother turned her back on me. I didn't know how I was going to repay her, but I promised I would.

My biggest fear was having to deliver my baby alone, but I tried my best to mentally prepare myself for it. I hated taking medicine because I used to watch how my mamma stayed high all the time, but once that pain became unbearable, I started begging for an epidural. I handled everything like a champ.

Two hours after arriving at the hospital, Laura Nicole entered the world, weighing in at 6 pounds, 3 ounces. I watched the nurses intensely wipe her down and take her vitals. When they finally laid my baby on my chest, I was so happy and couldn't stop crying. She was just perfect.

I didn't want to let her go with the nurses, but my body was so exhausted that I did not even remember falling asleep.

"Harper, she is so beautiful," I heard a voice say.

Is that my momma? I thought. *What is she doing here? Am I dreaming?*

Struggling to open my eyes, I fought myself to wake up. I glanced around the room and blinked my eyes a couple of times. I was trying to find any landmark that would remind me of my location. My head felt heavy, and I still couldn't move my legs. I sat up, placing two pillows behind my back.

Sitting in a chair next to Laura's bassinet was Mamma. Even behind the mask, I could see that she was crying. She rocked back and forth in the chair. She kept opening her mouth to speak, but no words came out.

"Mamma, what are you doing here?" I asked, feeling annoyed.

I didn't know how I was supposed to take her being there. Happy? Overjoyed?

"Harper, I know I have been mean to you, and sometimes, a disappointment as a mother, but I want you to know that I am sorry," she said. She rocked her body and rubbed her hands together in her lap.

"I didn't know how to be a mother, baby girl because I didn't have one. Everyone gave up on me when I started working in the streets. I never protected you, baby, not from Carlos and now, not from James. Seeing this baby, seeing how she is the splitting image of you, I think this is God giving me another chance to have a do-over. Only if you let me, of course."

Mamma stood up and walked over to the bed. She reached for my hand. At first, I hesitated, but I wasn't that strong. I had been waiting for my mamma to say words like that to me for years. So, like my Aunt

Laura said, when she apologized for her behavior, it was better late than never.

COVID-19 caused me to be in this hospital alone. I was constantly hearing about people dying every day on the news. It was a testament that life was too short.

I clasped her hand had back and looked up at her with tears streaming down my eyes.

"Harper, I am so sorry," she said. "Will you ever forgive me?"

I nodded, yes. Mamma and I embraced and cried for what seemed like an eternity. Once we were discharged, instead of going back to Aunt Laura's house, the baby and I went home with Mamma.

I am not going to lie, things just didn't miraculously get better, but there has been a lot of improvement. James had not been by, and I hadn't heard my mother on the phone with him. I guessed she was finally putting me first and that was the best birthday present in the world.

Now that Laura was here, life was harder than I thought it would be. I did have WIC, a program that gave me baby milk and basic food supplies. My social worker, Ms. Manuel, made sure I had a car seat, but that was pretty much it. I was 16 now and needed a job. Even though Vegas was not in complete lockdown anymore, every call center job that allowed me to work from home, required me having Wi-Fi. Mamma owed a bill, and we couldn't even get the free service that Cox was offering, so I struggled to find a job.

Mamma said it was not safe for me to work a fast food job or at Walmart because of Laura, and I agreed with her. My baby was too precious for me to bring any illness home to her.

I saw a lot of folks on Instagram, advertising that they had an Only Fans page, and I was desperately considering it. I could do it from my cellphone and didn't need to do too much. Men were always telling me how much they loved my red hair and eyes, so I might as well get paid for them to look at me.

The sound of someone pounding on my door interrupted my thoughts. Since James had stopped coming by, we did not have any visitors. I scooped Laura up and started down the stairs to open the door. She needed a bottle anyway, so I was going to knock out two birds with one stone.

"Harper, don't you bring that baby down here," Mamma said to me.

The pounding intensified as I continued down the stairs.

"I need to make her a bottle," I replied. "I will stay in the kitchen until whomever it is leaves."

Momma opened the door, and Mr. Davis, our landlord, pushed past her.

"Do you have a mask?" Mamma asked in disgust. "We have a new baby in the house, and we are protecting her from getting sick."

He whipped his mask out of his back pocket. "Christine, it's been months since you've paid rent!" Mr. Davis barked at my mamma. "When are you going to start paying? And I don't want to hear no Covid excuses either!"

I couldn't stand how that man stared at me or the way he talked to us.

"I haven't seen that hotshot around lately. He ain't paying the rent anymore?" he asked.

Mamma hadn't complained out loud to me about the lack of support from James, like she usually does, but I knew that we were struggling. That is why I was trying to figure out a way to make some money and fast. The landlord gave me the creeps.

"I am working on the rent, Clyde, and I told you this already," Mamma retorted back. Her voice was full of annoyance. "Isn't there something Sisolak signed, saying you can't put me out? You must want me or something?"

One thing about my mamma, she might not have been be book smart, but she was street smart. She could work her away around a man. I have witnessed her get our utilities cut back, groceries dropped off for free, and James had been paying rent for years.

Mamma was going to get him right one way or another.

Clyde rolled his eyes with disgust at my momma and shook his head.

"Naw, sweetheart," he replied. "You need to retire. You are in this predicament because what you have between your legs isn't working anymore. Now, that girl of yours..."

Before he could finish, Mamma blew up.

"GET THE FUCK OUT OF MY HOUSE!" she yelled. "ARE YOU TRYING TO GET ME TO SELL YOU MY DAUGHTER, FOOL? DON'T YOU EVER COME AT ME LIKE THAT AGAIN OR I WILL HAVE SOMEONE TAKE YOUR ASS OUT. DO YOU HEAR ME?"

Ever since Laura was born, Mamma had really been trying not to get upset or blow up at me, so I knew that Clyde must have really pissed her off.

Clyde rushed out the door, not saying another word. The man was hilarious if he thought I was going to sleep with him for no money. I figured since he wanted me so badly, let's see if he was going to put his money where his mouth was. He was going to be my first customer.

Stomping up the stairs, my mamma went to her room and slammed the door.

I wondered what she made her angrier – Clyde wanting me or him not wanting her anymore. I turned my attention back to feeding Laura and setting up my page on my phone.

Yalonda

As I sat in the car, I debated whether or not I should knock on the door. I was waiting to see if the door was going to open, and she would come outside on her own, but after three and a half hours, I had no such luck.

So, this is where James spent all his time? I thought. *He even had bills in his name over here!* I didn't know why, but I just wanted to meet the woman who took my husband from me. Literally.

I grabbed the envelope and put on my mask. All eyes were on me as I crossed the courtyard, but I kept my eyes fixated on the door. 328 was the apartment number, and I was out of breath after climbing those stairs.

I took a few deep breaths and quickly knocking on the door before I could change my mind.

It didn't take long for the door to open, but the person who opened it was not who I expected. She was a short, blond-haired white woman answered. Even though her body was athletic and youthful, her face was the total opposite. By the face, she looked like she was an older woman, at least close to 50. If this was Christine, according to James, she wasn't even 35 yet.

"How can I help you," the lady asked, appearing disgruntled.

"Hello," I said slowly. "Are you Christine?'

Hesitantly, she paused before glaring up at me.

"Do I know you?" she asked, her body language changing to hostile.

"No, you do not know me, but you do know my husband, James," I replied matter of factly.

"Husband?" The look of total shock spread over her entire face.

"Yes ma'am. May we talk inside?" I said, shifting my weight from one side to the other.

I didn't feel too comfortable standing at the door, especially not with the news I was about to deliver.

"No, we may not!" she said. "My grandbaby is lying down, and I do not want her exposed to too many folks with this virus going around."

"Oh my God! There really is a baby! Is Harper her mother?" I asked.

The mention of her daughter's name made Christine's face turn beet red.

"Where the fuck is James? And how do you know about my daughter and granddaughter?" she asked.

I handed her the envelope and tried my hardest to not explode.

You bitch! I wanted to scream in her face, but I was doing my best to keep my composure. It was her fault that my husband was never home with his family. I was standing there, justifying myself to this trailer trash ass bitch! It was her fault that my life was crumbling around me, including my finances.

Slowly, she opened the envelope and pulled out the pile of papers that were inside. She started with her NV Energy bill, followed by James' death certificate, pictures of Harper, and some printouts of text messages.

"James is dead?" she exclaimed, grasping her throat. "What happened? When! Where!"

She stepped back and opened the door all the way, finally letting me in. Following her, I closed the door behind me. The living room appeared dark and damp.

There, asleep on the couch, nestled in a blanket with a pillow beside her to prevent her from falling to the ground was the chunkiest baby I had ever seen.

Even in this dimly lit room, I could see how beautiful she was!

Christine was leaned against the wall, lost in the documents. I sat down in the chair next to the baby and just stared at her. Even in her sleep, she looked just like the girl in those pictures – red skin, hair, and all. If everything was true, she was my son's sister. I still debated with myself about if I was ever going to tell him.

"James died in a car accident. He was on his way to take you to the hospital when Harper was in labor, according to those text messages," I said.

"That long ago? No wonder he didn't call anymore! I thought it was because I told him that I knew what he did," Christine responded.

Silently, I nodded my head, yes.

"Did you get to the notes I printed?" Quickly, she started fumbling through the documents.

"Did you know the notes from an iPhone could be pulled up in your email? That's how I found all the information out about Harper. According to his notes, he was high one night and thought your daughter was me. According to him, there was a sexual encounter between the two of them." I stated all of this slowly. It was so hard spouting these words out loud, but it had to be said. "According to his notes, he didn't intentionally rape her. He was hallucinating and thought he was having sex with me. Since it happened, it had been driving him crazy up until the day he died."

I told her everything I knew or had found out that pertained to her and her daughter. When I got to the part about how James had a life insurance policy on the side for Harper, Christine was in utter shock!

My husband loved that little girl all up until the day he died and wanted the best for her. It took me months to be able to do this. After going through all of the pictures and notes in his phone, I learned that he didn't really care about Christine. It was his infatuation with this little girl that kept him around. If he could have had it his way, he would have brought her home to us a long time ago, but sometimes, life was not that easy.

I stood abruptly. I had been there long enough. I needed to get out of there. I was watching Christine cry and couldn't help myself from constantly staring at that baby. It all made me want to cry too, and the walls felt as if they were closing in around me.

"The last page of that packet is the information for Harper's life insurance. She can cash it out once she turns 21. The card attached is his lawyer's. Contact him for more information."

I didn't give her a chance to say anything else to me. I quickly opened the front door and left.

It took all of me to go to that woman's home, but now that I've done it, maybe my mind could relax. Finally, maybe I could get some rest and find some peace of my own.

Clyde

"See, man! Look at her. Shorty is bad!" I said.

Stone and I were sitting in my office, sipping on cognac. I sent him the link, but he said he couldn't open it. He had said something about not having a digital footprint if something happens.

I had been a fan of Red SunShyne for a few weeks now, and I had to admit baby girl was very entertaining. We sat online for hours, and she would act out scenes that the highest bidder requested. Not only was she beautiful, but Red prided herself on being a good listener and true to her word. For every fan I referred to her, she did whatever I asked for free. I even knocked down the balance her mother owed.

Stone was a friend of mine that used to move major drugs all over Vegas. He had since graduated from pushing pills to pushing girls, the younger, and the better. I figured being in the business he was in, he had a bunch of cliental he could refer to Red. Maybe he could get a sweet deal like she gave me.

I knew that she was older than he liked. His girls usually started around the age of eleven or twelve, but it didn't hurt to ask. I was running out of folks to share her with and was starting to get desperate.

I looked across the table, trying to read Stone's face, but he was expressionless and cold. When we were young, they nicknamed him "Stone Cold" because no matter what was going on, he never showed any emotion.

"What do you think?" I asked, lighting my cigar.

"Do you think you got any folks that may like her? If so, I have a referral code for them to use to see her at a discounted price."

I left out the part about how she could track that the referral came from me. You can never tell dudes everything because they could in turn cut me out of the deal. He could have her set him up with his own code. In the streets, you had to think it all the way through and be smarter than the average bear.

Stone finished off his drink with one gulp. He stood up, dapping my elbow with his.

"Send that link to Denise, so she can set up the account for me. Once she is done, I'll be in touch. Thanks, man. Good looking out."

Once he was gone, I couldn't stop smiling! Now that Stone was onboard, I'd never have to pay. I smiled as if I had just won the lottery and took another sip of my drink.

Christine

Christine. I am sorry that I hurt your

daughter. I am so sorry.

When I woke up from my dream, my body was
shaking. Ever since James' wife came by, I couldn't
stop thinking and dreaming about him. I assumed that
he was not contacting me because I stood up to him,
had showed him my power. Now, I knew the truth.
James had died trying to right the wrongs he had
caused my family, and it haunted me every night.

I got out of bed and headed downstairs to grab a bottle of water. Usually, I had a hard time keeping my fucking mouth shut, but I didn't tell Harper anything.

She knew too damn much because of me and my big mouth. I told her everything. She had to grow up so much faster because of my choices and mistakes. I hated it. Harper knew when I was on drugs, and she knew when I was working the streets. Ever since the birth of Laura, I had been using her as motivation to be different. I know I fucked up with Harper, but maybe I could make up for it by how we raised this baby.

She was innocent, and I wanted to keep her like that. It wasn't until I laid my eyes on my beautiful grandbaby that I realized why my daddy felt the way he did about Harper. He was trying to right his wrongs and correct the shortcomings he had had with me through Harper. That was totally what I wanted to do with Laura. She was not going to know any of my issues, unless it was in a teaching situation. This baby is going to make it.

I walked past Harper's room and heard voices coming through the door. I froze.

"You like that, Daddy?" I heard my daughter ask.

Who the hell is she talking too? I wondered. And with my grandbaby in there with her?

"Yes, Red, just like that!" I heard a grown man's voice respond.

Does she have someone in there?

After years in the sex industry, I knew exactly what those words meant, and I would be damned if that girl was going to go down the same path I went down. She would not allow men to take advantage of her.

When I pushed the door open, I couldn't believe what I was seeing. The baby was fast asleep in her bassinet next to the bed. Harper was standing in front of a laptop, playing with herself. There was a man, who appeared to be older than me on the screen, coaching her and jacking off.

Where the hell did this laptop even come from? And how was she able to be on the internet? We don't have Wi-Fi!

The pair were so wrapped up in each other, they didn't realize that I was standing there. It didn't take long for the dude to please himself and ejaculate all over the place.

"Oh, Red! I needed that baby," he replied, hooping and heaving.

"I am glad she was able to assist!" I said, startling the pair.

"Twan, I –I am going to call you back. My nanny just got here. See you later," Harper said, slamming the laptop shut.

"Mamma! Why are you coming into my room without knocking?" she asked.

I stood in my spot still in disbelief. She had the nerve to holler at me. *How did this happen? When did it happen?* I thought. I knew that with everything that had happened to Harper this past year, she had become jaded and a little closed off. I thought it was just her adjustment to motherhood.

I knew that we were struggling, but I was doing the best I could, so that Harper wouldn't have to do this! I wanted my daughter to meet a man who could make me feel something other than contempt or lust. I didn't want her selling her pussy via video chat! I knew that the world was changing, but Harper was different. She was so much better than this!

"What did you just say to me?" I asked in a calm, but stern tone. "I don't think I heard you correctly."

Harper backed up towards the bed, never breaking my gaze.

She wrapped a robe around herself, and sat down next to the baby.

"I am making me some money, Mamma." she responded matter-of-factly.

I moved to stand in front of her and placed my hands on my hips. "Girl! You know what I have been through to make some money? First, it starts off easy like this, but it always escalates to shit you can't control! What about your future, Harper? What about Laura?"

Harper's eyes pierced through me and responded in a cool, collected tone, "I am not you, Mamma."

"I have been doing this for months now, Mamma, and these dudes love me. I have money saved up to buy me a car, so I can stop walking with Laura in her stroller. I have it all mapped out, Mamma. So, you are right. I am thinking of my future. One of my clients gave me this computer and paid for the mobile hotspot, so I wouldn't have to work from my phone. He –"

"Wait, what? One of your clients? These dudes know where you live? Where you and your baby rest your heads?" I asked. I laugh4d out loud and started pacing.

"I am not crazy, Mamma. All of them don't know where I live, only Stone. He is different, Mamma. He doesn't want me to do this anymore, but if I am going to do it, he wanted to help me at least succeed. So, yeah, he came by here to drop off the computer and the hotspot. He is so beautiful, Mamma, and charming. Whenever we talk, he pays me to just listen. He cares about me, Mamma, for real."

"Girl, you are dumb as hell!" I exclaimed. "Don't nobody that you meet while selling pussy cares about you. They care about the service that you are providing, baby! Not you! How old is this clown, Harper? Why the hell would he want to save you? That fool is grooming you, dummy! You have a baby to think about, little girl, and I will be damned if you make the same mistakes I did. If you are going to stay here, you will be returning this laptop and get a real job. You are not going to be a HOE, HARPER! DO YOU HEAR ME?"

"I AM NOT A HOE, MAMMA! THAT IS YOU!"

Harper pushed me so hard that I flew into the wall.

"I am not selling my pussy. I am selling a service. You are just jealous, Mamma, that no one wanted you! They only wanted your pussy!" he spat at me with her chest heaving.

"Stone told me that you would try to keep me from him. He said that you were jealous that I was different. He told me that you were the enemy, leaving me in jail and choosing James over me. He said that the only reason you were so happy to take care of Laura now is because she was James' baby. It was something you were never able to give him no matter how hard you tried. He said that I shouldn't even be fucking with you, all the while I constantly defended you. But he was right! You are jealous of me! Bitch, I am not you!" she yelled.

Harper grabbed her phone and called someone as she ran down the stairs.

"Yes, I am okay," I heard her say. "You were right. Come get me. I can't stay here anymore."

Quickly, I grabbed Laura, clutching her to me with all my might. If Harper was going to leave, then so be it, but I would be damned if she took this baby with her.

Harper came back into the room and chuckled at me. She began gathering her things.

"You wanted a baby for James so badly, Mamma. You can have her. Stone told me you would try to hold her hostage. Hell! I shouldn't be taking care of a baby that came from a man who raped me – your man at that. So, fuck James; fuck Laura; and Mamma, most of all, fuck you."

Harper rushed out of the room with only a bag, that laptop, and her phone. She left me and the baby alone, never even kissing her good-bye.

Harper

I could feel the pounding of my heart beating in my ears as I sat on the curb, waiting for Stone to pick me up. I had been sitting there for well over two hours, trying to get my thoughts together about what exactly it was that I came to do. Part of me wanted to turn back around and go back into the house. I wanted to pick up my baby and lay with her, but I thought I went too far with Mamma.

Think. Think. Think girl! What if this dude doesn't come to pick me up? Where am I going to go? What am I going to do?

Mamma had come to the door twice, hollering my name but I ignored her.

That was over an hour and a half ago. After all the bullshit I witnessed her go through with these creeps she called men, I had to stand my ground – pull up or shut up. I wanted her to hurt as much as I did. That lady had hurt me!

She had walked in on James raping me and never did anything to protect me. That was the last straw for me! Then, not only did she not protect me, she allowed me to go jail and left me there.

When she came to the hospital and apologized, I thought I was good, but deep down, I wasn't. I just compartmentalized those feelings, like I did everything else. I was always making excuses for her.

That was until I found that envelope about James. I don't know where she got the information from, but that lady didn't even have the nerve to hide it! She just left it on her dresser in her room for the world to see. The worst part is that she could have gotten away with all of it if she had just left out Laura's shot records for me, like I asked. She made a big deal of being the one to hold onto all of our important papers, and that was not the problem. I just wished she hid that envelope, like she did everything else.

After reading the contents of the envelope, I had mixed feelings. First, I was elated to see that James was dead, but that elation went away once I read his printed text messages. He had written so many paragraphs about me. He talked about how he wished he could take me from Mamma, how he loved me so much. He said the only reason he stuck around was to protect me.

Those messages left me with mixed feelings. The entire time I knew James, I thought of him as my dad. He was caring and nurturing. He provided for me as best as he could. So, when he raped me...

MY GOD! I INSTANTLY HATED HIM!

It was wild to find out that he was the reason my mamma even came to the hospital when I had my baby and that he had confessed to her of what he did to me! According to Mamma, she was the reason he was no longer around. She just left out the part that she watched him rape me.

That was it. That was the icing on the cake for me. My mamma kept getting chances on top of chances to make things better with me, but she didn't care.

Stone was right. When I had Laura, it made her feel like she was on top of the world because she had a piece of James. After I read those messages, I couldn't even lie. I started looking at Laura differently. I started having this uncomfortable feeling of jealousy for my own daughter. My mamma never took her time with me, but she was the best grandma in the world to Laura.

At first, I was confident that it was because Laura gave her a second chance with me, but after talking it out with Stone, he gave me another perspective. I even gave mamma an opportunity tonight to apologize for James and the policy I found, but she didn't say anything about it! She just sat hopped up, making sure she grabbed that baby. Well, since Mamma loved Laura so much, she could have her!

I was going to prove everyone wrong! I was going to show everybody that I was worth something. I WAS GOING TO BE THE TRIUMPHANT ONE! I was going to be the one to have my cake and eat it too.

"I heard somebody needs a ride?" asked a voice.

Without even looking up, I smiled, knowing that I finally had a chance to escape. The sound of Stone's music made me happy, as I gathered my things and stood up.

"Hi, baby," I said, getting in the car and kissing him full on the lips. "I thought you forgot about me."

I heard my mamma yelling my name again, telling me to come back. *As always, Mamma, you show up too little too late for me*, I thought.

"Sweetness, I could never do that," he assured me. "I was a little tied up."

I looked out my window in the direction of my apartment.

"Are you sure you are ready to leave this place?" he asked me firmly. "Are you ready to come home to your real family?"

His eyes were so sincere and serious, but his tone turned me on.

"Yes, baby," I answered him. "I am ready to go home."

He flashed a smile at me and held my hand, as we pulled away from the curb.

From the pen of: *Nicsia*

Denise

This little girl is lazy as hell, I thought to myself in disgust.

When I walked into the condo, her stuff was strewn all over the living room. I shook my head, picking up items and throwing them into a pile by the bedroom door. Harper had been here for a little over two weeks, and she seemed to be settling in just fine. My only issue with her was that her hygiene habits were horrible.

I had been getting to know Harper by pretending that I was Stone, and I felt sorry for the girl. She was dealt a terrible hand, and just like any other liar, I had really started to believe that if we got her out of that house, we would be saving her.

I gained her trust by only chatting with her, not via video. I never asked her for any sexual favors or advances. I offered her money for the baby and her expenses. It didn't take long to break her down. Finally, I got her to give me her address, so that Stone could drop off a laptop and hotspot to her. I knew that once she saw Stone in person and realized he was the face behind our awesome conversation that it wouldn't take long for her to come home to us, and I was right!

Literally, a week later, she was calling his phone and the rest was history. Now that she was here, Harper was really starting to get on my damn nerves!

What was $\mathcal{I}$ suppose to do?

Every time I came by, I had to remind her to take a shower and to wash her hair. She was a little older than the girls, so I thought she would be easier to manage, but her ass was getting on my damn nerves.

Sitting down on the couch, I texted Stone: **Here.** After a few moments, Stone appeared. He came out of the bedroom and closed the door behind him.

Sometimes, days like today, this shit got on my damn nerves! Stone would bring the new girls to my house and I would stay with the rest of them in the big house. I hated having to watch how he broke them in. He would have sex with them and pretend he was their man.

"Hey, you," Stone said, wrapping a towel around his naked hips.

I understood how these girls fell for him. He was fine as hell. His chest was chiseled and he had the prettiest smile. Grown women threw themselves at him all the time, so what kind of effect do you think he had on these young ones?

His fingertips traced my left cheek, as he leaned in and kissed me tenderly on the lips. I took in a deep breath. His kiss was perfect. It felt as if my chest was caving in, and my heart was going to erupt like a volcano.

In a sultry manner, he licked my lips with his tongue. I exhaled, releasing my tender breath into his awaiting mouth. Our tongues played a tug of war. Before I could turn my body so that it could be one with him, I felt a pair of small hands running across my quickly hardening nipples. The scent of Harper's mound lingered in his mouth, bringing me back to reality.

"Hold on, baby. We need to chill out," he said.
He stared at me intensely, rubbing his fingertips over my breasts through my shirt. Oh, how I longed to feel him again!

"You are so beautiful," Stone whispered. He stood up, rubbing his erected tool underneath the towel. "I know you are frustrated, but I am getting everything together, baby. She is almost ready. I promise."

I didn't know how he had such a hold on me, but he did. He was like the pied piper, using his dick to make women conform to his every will, me included.

I really didn't know what to expect when I got that text message from Stone, telling me to meet him at the spot, but I was ready to go. I needed a break from the big house and all those girls!

Some days, I was ready to leave all this madness behind and go find a regular man to have a normal life. Some days, it was hard for me to remember what exactly the word "normal" meant.

I hadn't been sleeping much. I was tossing and turning, upset about having to keep this crazy secret about this crazy life I was living. I was ready to leave all the foolery in the past, and enjoy whatever it was that the future may hold. Then, Stone would kiss or touch me the way he did, and I was trapped, sliding back down the rabbit hole.

I knew I was a grown-ass woman, but something about me always attracted the bad boys.

"So, what is going on, baby? Why was it so important for me to come by and not call?" I asked him.

Stone didn't like a paper trail, and he especially hated technology. He had spent enough time in jail and had read enough books to know that texts and calls were the easiest ways to be traced. Whenever he had a big idea or plan, he always wanted to speak face-to-face.

According to him, it was the safest way.

He grabbed a bottle of water out of the fridge. Stone sat down at the kitchen table, taping the mat beside him so I would join him.

Obediently, I got up and sat across from him.

Taking a sip of water, Stone looked at me across the table, emotionless.

"Everything has been confirmed with Black," he said, "and once he has secured payment from all of the men, we are going to test Harper out.

I figured if we brought them back here and let them run a train on her, not only will we be making money, but breaking her in at the same time.

She has already been working, so she won't be hard to get in order. After that, we can start selling her on the street to the highest bidder. I think we can get more for her by prepaid customers than having her walk the track. Do you agree?"

I guess by the look on my face, he knew I was in complete awe on how he came up with a strategic plan for each girl. He never ceased to amaze me.

"Yes, baby, I think that plan is amazing," I said. "Just let me know what you need from me between now and then."

Harper

Miami? Mexico?

I laid on the couch with my head propped up on pillow, daydreaming about our nearing vacation. Once we came off this crazy ass lockdown, we were out of here! Stone had been very vague about the destination. The furthest place I had ever been was Cali when my Papa took me to Disneyland.

How old was I? Seven? Nine?

That shit was crazy! I ain't done nothing! After Papa had his stroke and ended up in that home, the only person I had was my crazy ass mama, and she never had any money! But that was about to change. Stone promised me the world and I was more than willing to take him up on his offer. The thought of traveling the world with that beautiful man made my heart flutter every time it came to mind. I was so lucky. Who would have ever thought he would have picked me to be his girl? Me! The half-breed mutt-girl, who ain't know who her own damn Daddy was could land a man like that?!

I was taking in my beautiful setting, listening to the Neo Soul station on Spotify and trying to learn some of the old songs that were playing. Neo Soul was Stone's favorite genre of music. I didn't want to appear as young as I was while we were on vacation, or once he started taking me around his family.

Lost in my thoughts, I did not hear the keys unlocking the front door. I was grinning from ear-to-ear when Stone entered the apartment, but my grin quickly faded when I realized that he had four guys behind him.

"Hey there, pretty girl," he said with a soft smile on his lips.

"Someone is happy to have me back home I see," he said, leaning in to brush a quick kiss against my lips.

I hurried up to pull the throw blanket up over my body. I tried tucking my body down behind the oversized pillows on the couch. I wasn't wearing anything but a pair of boy shorts and a sports bra. I didn't know he was going to bring company home with him. Stone hadn't brought anyone besides his sister, Denice, to the house, so I was totally caught off guard.

From the pen of: *Nina*

He must've sensed my nervousness. Stone gestured for the guys to take a seat in the dining room as he sat down next to me, rubbing my hand.

Even though I trusted this man with my life, the energy in the room was making me uncomfortable. The hairs on the back of my neck stood up and my body had a sudden chill.

"Pretty girl, these are a few of my friends. I told them about you, and they offered me top dollar to meet you," he said in a gentle baritone.

Top dollar? Did this dude just say what I think he said?

I shook my head, looking at Stone, then turned my attention to the men seated at the dining room table, cheesing like they just won the lottery. They looked the kind of guys Mama used to be on the corner with when I would go looking for her when I was little.

"Black, we can't see her, man. Gotta make sure she worth the five stacks," the pudgy one said.

He stood up, rubbing his hand across his crotch. I guessed he was waiting for me to get up.

My chills turned into a full-blown round of the shakes and my head started to hurt really badly.

OMG! Did he sell me to these guys? How much is five stacks? Five hundred or five thousand, and who the fuck is Black?

Not giving me an opportunity to speak, Stone grabbed my hand, looking me dead in the eyes.

"Don't embarrass me now, Harper," he said, exposing the gun at his waist with his other hand. "I need you to stand up, go to the guest room, and get into the shower. Leave on the towel and wait on the bed like a good girl.

When you are ready, call my name and I will send them in one-by-one. I need you to make them feel good, like you make me feel good. Okay? I have been bragging about you, baby. They just want to make sure that you are everything that I said you are. Now, be a good girl and do what I say. You hear me?"

Still holding my hand with a tight grasp, he pulled me slowly but firmly. The tears that had welled up in my eyes finally released and rolled down my face.

This man had claimed to love me and promised to never hurt me, but he really sat there, telling me that he sold me! He knew how I felt about pimps and prostitutes! He knew everything about me! *Why the hell is he doing this to me?*

Mama always said that if a man seemed too perfect, it was because there was a dirty secret he was hiding and needed his perfection to overpower it. After a while, his representative will go away and the real him would come out. I always blew her off when she spouted her hood parables, but right now, all of her words were ringing out in between my ears.

"Stop that shit, Harper. Now, go wash up. Make sure you use that smell-good body wash in there and wash your hair. Got to make sure you are fresh and clean for our guests, okay?"

He still spoke in his normal, soothing tone. Stone pushed me in the direction of the guest room, snatching the blanket from around me, exposing my barely clad body.

I knew that if I went into that room, I might never make it out because they were going to have to kill me before they raped me.

Did they know I was only sixteen?

I guess if it didn't matter to Stone, then it damn sure must not have mattered to them.

"Yea, my G. Her ass is fat like you said," the tall, light-skinned one said. "I got shotgun!" he exclaimed to the other guys at the table.

I wanted to scream and cry, but this was not the time for that. If I could pull this shit off, I could to do that later, but not now. Right now, I had to save my life.

I turned my attention back to Stone, trying to tune their voices out my head. Flashing him a soft smile, I turned all my feminine wiles on, hoping my pheromones would work in my favor at this moment. All my life, my mamma taught me the game that I had to use from time to time, but this was a moment when I had to pay attention and keep my cool if this shit was going to work.

"I got you, baby," I said before I leaned in to hug him and who would have thought? He opened his arms to embrace me, giving me a small window of opportunity to save my life. I hurried in and tugged the gun out of his waistband.

What the fuck!" he yelled, but I was too quick. I had possession of the gun, and the bad part about being raised in the projects and having a hoe for a mamma, I knew exactly how to use it.

Knowing from the weight and the bulge at the bottom, I knew it was loaded. I held the gun firmly, cocked it, and aimed it directly at Stone.

"Nigga, I thought you said she was with this!" the pudgy one yelled out to Stone.

"I am on papers and don't have time for no bullshit," he said, while inching towards the door.

The tall, light-skinned one stood up and said, "I am not going anywhere until I get some pussy or my bread back, period."

In that instance I knew, I was going to have to shoot and maybe kill someone tonight.

"Bitch! I told you not to embarrass me!" Stone hollered out, lunging towards me.

Stepping back, I took the shot, closing my eyes as the blast from the gun rang out in the air.

Quickly, I opened my eyes and saw Stone falling to the ground, wailing out in pain. He was clutching the area where the bullet landed in his right leg.

"This bitch is crazy! And we on the strip. Them boys will be here real quick!" yelled the pudgy one, rushing to the door. The other two quiet ones were running out as well.

I focused my attention now on the tall one, who was still standing there. I gazed up at him, pointing the gun, and said, "I think it's best if you left too."

He stood there, glaring at me, daring me to shoot him. I was tired of men trying to take advantage of me. I cracked my neck and let off another blast in his direction. This time, I missed, but that dude was not crazy. He rushed out the door, slamming it behind him.

"BITCH, YOU GOT ME SO FUCKED UP!" Stone spat, grabbing my neck from behind and catching me off guard.

I tried to fight him with all my might. As I tried to break free from his grasp, I dropped the gun.

"GET YOUR HANDS OFF OF ME, STONE!" I screamed, kicking him in his leg.

Stone screamed out in pain and flung me onto the kitchen island. I scanned the room and tried to find

something I could use as a weapon. I spotted the knife
set on the counter. I lunged to grab one, but not before
Stone charged at me. He repeatedly punched me in the
back of my head. "Bitch, I loved you! How could you
do this shit to me?" he yelled, punching me dead in the
middle of my back.

"I am sorry," I exclaimed, crying uncontrollably.
If someone had told me that when I met Stone, he was
eventually going to be the one trying to kill me, I would
have told them, "Yeah right."

"Bitch, did you think you would be able to leave
me like that, huh? After everything I have done for your
punk ass? You got me and the game fucked up," Stone
exclaimed, throwing me against the kitchen counter
again. "You need to learn how dangerous it is to fuck
with grown men. That is why you are in the situation
you are in, playing like you are fucking innocent."

What was I suppose to do?

Using the little bit of power left inside of me, I grabbed the biggest knife. Stone had tears streaming from his eyes. His face was full of rage. He lunged at me, trying to get the knife out of my hand, but he was too late. With all my might, I pushed the knife as far into his stomach as I could, turning it to the right. I could hear my papa's voice in the back of my head, "Harper poo, in the event that you have to protect yourself, never turn the knife after penetration. If you do, your attacker will die, and we don't want that, do we?"

When I was little, that scared the hell out of me, and it's the main reason why I only stabbed James. But, this fool? After everything he had done to me? I turned the knife to the left and could feel the life escape from Stone's body. He collapsed onto the floor.

In the distance, I could hear the sounds of police sirens coming closer. Part of me wanted to run, but where was I going to go? Mentally and physically, I was exhausted, so I laid down next to Stone and waited.

Ni'Cola

"Hello," I grumbled into the phone. It was 3:30 in the morning, and I had just gotten to sleep. I had been up working all night and was trying to get some rest before I had to get on the road in a few hours. I was going to Savannah to spend time with my daughter for the weekend. It was a much-needed break.

"Hi, Ms. Mitchell. I am so sorry to call you late like this, but Harper is in trouble," said Ms. Manuel, Harper's old social worker. I remembered her soft voice instantly through the phone.

I sat up straight in the bed, fighting my body to wake all the way up! I hadn't heard from Harper in months! I gave Ms. Manuel money to buy a car seat and diapers for the new baby, but that was the last I had heard from her.

"I don't know the complete story, but Harper was arrested a few hours ago," Ms. Manuel said. "She is currently being held at the juvenile facility, but I am not sure how long they are going to keep her there this time."

It took a moment for me to comprehend everything that Ms. Manuel had just said to me.

Did she just say that Harper was in trouble again? What about the baby? What about her family? Did she hurt her mother?

"So, this is serious? What is she being charged with?" I asked.

I rushed into the bathroom and rinsed warm water over my face. I listened as the case worker replayed the conversation that she had with law enforcement.

She was speaking so fast and was all over the place; I was so confused.

"Ms. Manuel, calm down," I said, trying to bring sense to the situation. "She killed a pimp? He beat her up? She was on the strip when it happened? I know her mother used to work the streets. Do you think she sold her?"

"As much as I have grown to despise her mother, I really do not think she has anything to do with it this time. Since the birth of the baby, she seemed to have been getting better," Ms. Manuel answered.

"Well, as much as I love to hear a parent has been getting better, sometimes, they did too little, and their responses were too late for how far gone they pushed their kids," II responded sarcastically.

I caught my tone and apologized for being rude.

"Thank you so much for the information" I said to her. "I am just frustrated by the entire situation. Her mom is not the only one to blame. There are a lot of folks who dropped the ball in regard to this child... including me. I am going to book a flight to come out there in the morning. At least we found her!"

I texted my daughter, Diamond, and gave her a brief explanation of what was going on. I told her I would have to come down to visit her the following weekend and canceled our plans.

I rushed around my house, pulling on a pair of jeans and a "God is Dope" sweatshirt. I threw some things in a duffel bag and mentally prepared myself.

What was I suppose to do?

My shoulders heaved when I finally sat down at my desk to find a flight.

"Dear Lord in heaven, please watch over Harper," I whispered a quick prayer as I looked for flights.

From the pen of: *Nicola*

Epilogue

*B*uzzzzzzz. The alarm rang out as my cell door opened up. I placed my hands behind my back and waited until the guard nodded her approval for me to step out.

"You have a visitor," the officer informed, nudging for me to move.

Mamma had been here every week with Laura. She was actually being a great support system, trying to convince me that everything was going to be okay. This time, however, it was different. I was being charged with third degree murder as an adult and the sentencing had a minimum of 20 years!

Where does that leave me with Laura? I wondered almost every night. *Does that leave her with my mamma? Will this case make my mamma relapse? Will my daughter even know me or care to know me once I'm released?*

There were so many things running through my head every night as I laid in bed. Once I got to the visitation room, I was shocked to see who was sitting there. It was Ms. Ni'cola!

I had started ignoring her calls when I moved back in with my mamma. I knew she wouldn't understand my decisions. My life was complicated. I was too ashamed to tell her that even though she did so much for me to get out and start my life over again, I went back to my mom.

If she knew that I was here, she knew about the charges. How was I going to explain all of this to her? How would I make her understand that I was not a bad person?

"Peace, Queen!" she said softly and smiled at me. "How are you doing?"

Her smile was the same, but her eyes looked tired.

"Pumpkin, I've been looking all over for you," she said. "I kept calling you. I thought you had me blocked. You stopped posting on social media. Did I do something to upset you? What happened, Harper?"

Just like always, Ms. Ni'cola's voice was so soothing and caring. I sat there for only a second, rocking back and forth. I crossed and uncrossed my arms in front of me.

I took in a deep breath and just let it all out. I told her everything. Never interrupting, she listened silently with tears streaming down her face.

Once I finished, I sighed and looked her dead in the eyes. "Now that I've told you everything, Ms. Ni'cola, can you tell me this?"

I sat up straight in the chair and she nodded at me. "Of course," she replied. "You can ask me anything."

Barely over a whisper, I asked, "What was I supposed to do?"

Meet Ni'cola Mitchell

L'Oréal Paris 2019 Women of worth Ni'cola Mitchell, Founder of Girls Who Brunch Tour, is a

Best-Selling Author who made the Forbes List as a Change Maker in 2019 and Black Enterprise 2015 as one of the 5-Follow Worthy Bloggers to Watch. Through her independent publishing company NCM Books, Ni'cola published numerous titles which have been featured on various best-selling lists throughout the country. Much of her work revolves around complex relationship issues and Mitchell's compulsive desire to see women overcome challenges.

Ni'cola is the owner of Strategic Connections Plus a start-up business consulting firm that facilitates the growth of small business. She has penned 17 novels, published 125 titles, and has helped over 1k authors and independent publishers publish their books successfully.

Ni'cola has also received the 2020 George H. W. Bush's Daily Points of Light Award and the 2020 Civility for the Girl Child Initiative Honoree. As a victim of domestic violence, Ni'cola Mitchell understood first-hand how at-risk youth are significantly less likely to successfully transition into adulthood due to a lack of resources and opportunity. Her own past led her to create Girls Who Brunch, a non-profit that combats this cultural epidemic by addressing low-income communities, and sponsoring girls in foster care, as well as sex trade victims and teen mothers.

Through mentorship, workshops, STEAM training, and panel facilitations, Girls Who Brunch teaches different ways of thinking that ultimately enables at-risk girls to succeed and flourish. Through her work with Girls Who Brunch, she has positively impacted and equipped over 25K girls nationwide on ground and virtually.

Reviews

If you enjoy this story, Please leave a review. This is how others will know to take the time and read a novel from the pen of Ni'cola! Thank you so much! Just click on the following link:

amzn.to/2VoaaB6

Once you finish reading this story, I am asking all of you to take a moment and process what would you have done, if you were in Harper's situation.

Please share your thoughts via a 2 minute video on social media tagging me at the any of the social media outlets below using the hashtag #WhatwasIsupposedtodo.

Follow me on!
Instagram.com/Mz_Nicola
Facebook.com/MsNicola
Twitter.com/MsNicola
www.IAmNicola.com
www.girlswhobrunchtour.com

Follow us

on all social networks

@GIRLSWHOBRUNCHTOUR

Top 5 National Resources for Girls

Suicide Prevention

https://suicidepreventionlifeline.org/

Stop Bulling

https://www.stopbullying.gov

Pregnancy Assistance

https://optionline.org/

Rape and sexual abuse Hotline

https://www.rainn.org/

Human Trafficking Prevention

https://humantraffickinghotline.org/

Made in the USA
Las Vegas, NV
17 August 2021